Bumper
of Horror

Gyles Brandreth

Illustrated by Roy Bentley,
David Farris and David Simonds

MADCAP

Published in Great Britain in 1997 by
Madcap Books, André Deutsch Ltd,
106 Great Russell Street, London, WC1B 3LJ, England
André Deutsch Ltd is a subsidiary of VCI plc

Text copyright © 1997 Madcap Books/Gyles Brandreth
Illustrations copyright © Roy Bentley, David Farris
and David Simonds

A catalogue record for this title is available
from the British Library

ISBN 0 233 99084 4

Contents

GHASTLY RHYMES

SPOOKTACULAR JOKES

The Monster Market

From Monday to Saturday, from midnight until dawn, the Monster Market opens its doors to all kinds of monsters and spooks. It sells awide range of the goods that all spooks love, including Count Dracula's favourite breakfast cereal, Readyneck, and a good selection of wines and spirits in the drinks department. Come on in and join the monster fun!

GHOUL: I think I'll buy something for lunch.
MONSTER: How about some ghoulash?

Who appears on the front of horror magazines?
The cover ghoul.

GHOST: I think I fancy some foreign food.
MONSTER: How about spooketti?

What should a monster do if he loses one of his hands? *Go to the second hand department of the Monster Market!*

GREEN MONSTER: Do you sell toilet water here?
MONSTER ASSISTANT: Yes, sir. We bottle it from our very own toilets.

What kind of flour do short elves buy?
Elf-raising flour

ZOMBIE: Oh, good, I see they've got some Christmas decorations on sale. I love eating them!
MUMMY: I had some last Christmas but they gave me tinselitis.

What's the difference between a monster and an apple?
Just try peeling a monster!

SPOOK: That trolley's moving all by itself!
GHOUL: No it's not – the invisible man is pushing it.
SPOOK: He looks a real idiot.
GHOUL: Don't be so mean. Can't you see he's not all there?

LADY MONSTER: I'm looking for something to make my rock cakes light.
MONSTER ASSISTANT: I'm afraid we don't sell petrol, madam.

Why does the Monster Market's butcher keep bandages under the counter?
To sell with chops and cold cuts.

GHOST: I'm not buying any more frozen food.
GHOUL: Why not?
GHOST: A zombie bent over the freezer yesterday and five fish fingers jumped out and strangled him!

Can you tell the difference between a lemon and a blue monster?
The lemon is yellow.

MONSTER ROBOT: Do you sell little bits of metal?
MARKET MANAGER: Yes, we do.
MONSTER ROBOT: Good – it's my staple diet.

Dr Frankenstein has invented a new kind of breakfast food. He crossed an electric organ with a chicken, and now the Monster Market sells Hammond eggs.

SPOOK: That monster over there has pedestrian eyes.
GHOUL: Pedestrian eyes?
SPOOK: Yes, they look both ways before they cross.

What did the skeleton take for his cough?
Coffin drops.

MOTHER GHOST: What would you like to eat with your meat?
BABY GHOST: Grave-y!

MRS MONSTER: Can you stop my husband biting his nails?
DR FRANKENSTEIN: I could knock his teeth out . . .

ZOMBIE: I can't think what to buy my wife for her birthday.
SPOOK: Why not buy her a corset so that she can keep her ghoulish figure?

What did the short-sighted ghost buy at the Monster Market?
Spooktacles.

MRS MUMMY: My son insists on eating biscuits in bed.
MRS GHOUL: He must be one of those crummy mummies.

Where were the Monster Market's customers when the lights went out?
In the dark.

What did the monster buy for pudding?
Leeches and scream.

ADVERT: At the request of the sea monsters, the Monster Market now stocks fish and ships and, for mermaids' breakfasts, mermalade.

What did the Computer Monster steal from the Monster Market?
Frozen silicon chips.

SPOOK: How can you tell the difference between a monster that's asleep and a monster that's awake?
ZOMBIE: With most monsters it's difficult to tell.

Two lady monsters met whilst out shopping. "Your little ghoul's grown!" said one, looking at the other's daughter.

"Oh yes," said the proud mother. "She's certainly gruesome."

What do ghosts buy to put in their coffee?
Evaporated milk.

GHOUL: You should keep better control of your little boy. He just bit me on the ankle.
VAMPIRE: That's only because he couldn't reach your neck.

How can you tell the difference between a monster and a banana at the supermarket?
Pick it up. If you can't lift it it's probably a monster.

WITCH: That zombie over there just bit my leg!
GHOUL: Did you put something on it?
WITCH: No, he seemed to like it just as it is.

WITCH: I think I'll buy some spinach. It's good for you – it will put colour in your cheeks.
WIZARD: But I don't want green cheeks.

What did the dragon say when he saw St George walk into the Monster Market?
Not more tinned food!

What did E.T's mum say when he got home?
Where on earth have you been? I hope you brought the shopping from the Monster Market.

Why did the little monster push her father in the Monster Market's deep freeze?
Because she wanted frozen pop.

What happened when the abominable snowman sneezed in the Monster Market?
Everyone ran for cover.

GHOUL: Why were you sacked from your job at the Monster Market?
SPOOK: Sickness.
GHOUL: You were ill?
SPOOK: No – the sight of me made the manager sick.

When is the Monster Market like a boat?
When it has a sale.

GHOST: Have you got something to make sure that I lie absolutely flat in bed?
MARKET MANAGER: I think you need a spirit level.

What vegetables did the werewolf buy to go with his bones?
Marrows.

SPECIAL OFFER: For the older invisible ghost who is beginning to show –
Vanishing Cream.

FIRST WITCH: Have you tried one of those new paper cauldrons?
SECOND WITCH: Yes.
FIRST WITCH: Did it work?
SECOND WITCH: No, it was tearable.

Which fruit does the Monster Market stock especially for vampires?
Blood oranges.

What was the invisible sales manager's motto?
What you don't see you don't get.

What's the only kind of cake that monsters don't buy?
Cakes of soap.

Why did the monster comedian buy one hundred Oxo cubes?
He wanted to make a laughing stock of himself.

GHOUL: I'd like a packet of yeast and a tin of furniture polish.
MARKET MANAGER: Aha – you want to rise and shine!

What do you do with a green ghost?
Wait until he's ripe.

Why did the two one-eyed monsters fight in the Monster Market?
Because they didn't see eye to eye.

Why did the monster buy a light-bulb for lunch?
He felt in need of light refreshment.

WITCH: Shall I buy black or white candles?
GHOUL: Which burn longer?
WITCH: Neither, they both burn shorter.

How do you make a monster sandwich?
You go to the Monster Market and buy a **huge** *loaf* . . .

A little monster came home from school in tears. "All the children laugh at me!" he sobbed.

"Why, dear?" asked his mother.

"They say I have a big head."

"They don't know what they're talking about," reassured his mother. "Now would you go to the Monster Market and get me some groceries? We need six blood oranges, three pounds of potatoes, three tins of bat food, a large packet of minced worms in zombie slime, a box of dried cockroaches and two dozen dead frogs."

"Where's the shopping basket?" asked the little monster, looking for it.

"I forgot," said the mother monster. "The handles broke and I threw it away. Why don't you use your school cap to carry the shopping instead?"

The Creepy Kitchen

The Creepy Kitchen is the most popular restaurant in the ghost town. It caters for everyone – so pull up a chair, tuck in and enjoy yourself!

What happened when the Creepy cook stole some rhubarb?
He was put in custardy.

The Creepy Kitchen serves up some very strange meals, which sometimes confuse the diners. "Waiter, waiter," called one of them. "There's a hand in my soup."
    "That's not your soup, sir," explained the waiter, "that's the finger bowl."

GHOST: I live entirely on a diet of onions and garlic, and I'm so lonely!
SPOOK: No wonder!

DR FRANKENSTEIN: I had some uranium for lunch at the Creepy Kitchen today.
IGOR: Was it good?
DR FRANKENSTEIN: No – it gave me atomic ache.

Chaos at the Creepy Kitchen! A ghoul swallowed a cigarette lighter that was dropped in his soup. Fortunately he spat it out, so now he's delighted.

What do you call the ghost standing in the corner of the Creepy Kitchen with a sausage on his head? *A head banger.*

Should you eat mashed spiders in frog sauce on an empty stomach? *No – it's polite to eat it on a plate.*

How does Frankenstein eat his dinner? *He bolts it down.*

A zombie swallowed a watch last night at the Creepy Kitchen. It was a time-consuming business.

Why doesn't it cost much to take Dracula out for dinner? *Because he eats necks to nothing.*

Why do the spooks go to the Creepy Kitchen at 11 a.m.?
For a coffin break.

What should you expect if you call unexpectedly on a witch at lunchtime?
Pot luck.

What's the most popular pudding at the Creepy Kitchen?
Ice scream.

How did the monster snowman feel after eating an atomic-hot curry?
Abominable.

How can the Creepy Chef tell if he's had a hairy monster in the fridge?
There is fur in the butter.

A noisy little purple monster walked into the Creepy Kitchen. "What do you like to eat, Miss Spell?" he yelled at a witch, drawing up a chair at her table.

"Frogs' legs and snails," said the witch.

"And how about you?" shouted the noisy little purple monster, turning to where Count Dracula was sipping his soup.

"Human blood," said the Count.

"What do you like eating, Mr Ghoul?" yelled the noisy monster, dancing on a table.

"I just love eating noisy little purple monsters," said the ghoul.

"Oh," whispered the little purple monster, "you don't see many of *them* these days!"

How do ghosts like their drinks served in August? *Ice ghoul*.

What do little devils drink?
Demonade.

WITCH: I'm never coming to this restaurant again! My friend here has just swallowed a frog!
WAITER: Does she feel ill?
WITCH: Ill? She'll croak at any minute!

Why do skeletons always drink milk?

BECAUSE IT'S GOOD FOR THE BONES!

BECAUSE IT'S GOOD FOR THE BONES!

Did you hear about the ghost who was so thin you could see right through him?

Which little monster can eat everything in the Creepy Kitchen in ten minutes flat?
A goblin.

GHOUL: Waiter, waiter, you've got your sleeve in my soup!
GHOST WAITER: It's all right, sir, there's no arm in it.

What do you get if you cross a spook and a bag of crisps?
A snack that goes crunch in the night.

Knock, knock.
Who's there?
Betty.
Betty who?
Betty doesn't know what's on the menu at the Creepy Kitchen.

What's Count Dracula's favourite snack?
A fangfurter.

How does Frankenstein sit when he's dining at the Creepy Kitchen?
Bolt upright.

What's wrapped in greaseproof paper and runs round Paris at midday scaring people?
The Lunchpack of Notre Dame.

GHOST: Waiter, waiter, I think there's a monster hiding in my gravy.
WAITER: How do you know that, sir?
GHOST: Because it's *really* lumpy.

A Menacing Monster walked into the Creepy Kitchen. "Crocodile and chips to take away," he ordered. "And make it snappy."

Why doesn't Count Dracula like eating in restaurants?
He worries about getting a steak through the heart.

What did Tarzan say when the werewolf chewed his leg at the Creepy Kitchen?
Aaaaaah-eeeeeee-aaaah-eeeeee-aaaaahhh!!

Who visits the Creepy Kitchen after dark and goes chomp, chomp, aaagh?
A vampire with a bad tooth.

Which pub do miserable monsters go to for a drink?
The Horse and Gloom.

What's the best way of attracting the waiter at the Creepy Kitchen?
Scream!

What did the barman say to the spook who asked for a vodka?
Sorry, but we don't have a licence to serve spirits.

What do monsters eat at sea?
Fish and ships.

What did the vampire say when he found that there was nothing on the menu but thistles?
Thistle have to do.

A tiny green monster walked in to the Creepy Kitchen, sat down and ordered a cup of tea. He'd only been there five minutes when he noticed a huge, hairy, orange monster licking his lips. Then the orange monster began to sharpen his knife and growl quietly.

"Help!" said the little monster to the waiter. "Is he safe?"

"I'd say he was a lot safer than you are."

What is a beetroot?
A potato with high blood pressure?

Who lays the eggs for the Creepy Kitchen?
The poultry-geists.

What do witches like to eat for breakfast?
Rice Krispies because they go snap, cackle and pop.

What do witches like best for lunch?
Real toad in the hole.

What's the difference between a two-tonne yellow monster and a biscuit?
You can't dip the monster in your cocoa.

What do you call a monster with meat and potatoes on his head?
Stew.

What happened when the abominable snowman
bought a curry?
He melted.

What was on the Creepy Kitchen's menu the day
after the police called round?
I arrest stew.

"Waiter, waiter, is this tea or coffee?" asked the
ghost. "It's vile – it tastes like bleach."

"It must be tea, sir. Our coffee tastes like
washing-up liquid."

Eerie Corner

Eerie Corner is a street corner in the Ghost Town where all the monsters and spooks and ghouls love to meet for a chat and pass the time of night. Why not hang around with them and listen to the latest gossip?

PHANTOM: Why are you limping?
SPOOK: I went for a swim last week and a crocodile bit my foot off.
PHANTOM: Which one?
SPOOK: I've no idea – they all look the same to me.

Who will haunt the graveyard when the spooks go out on strike?
The skeleton crew.

Did you hear about the monster who went shoplifting?
He was crushed under Woolworths.

MRS MONSTER: My husband wants me to buy him an electrical gadget for his birthday.
MRS GHOUL: How about an electric chair?

ZOMBIE: Did you hear about the vampire who climbed Mount Everest?
SPOOK: No, I didn't.
ZOMBIE: Neither did I.

What do you get if you cross Robbie Fowler with a monster?
I'm not sure, but when it gets into the penalty area no one tries to stop it.

What do orange, smooth-skinned monsters have that no one else has?
Baby orange, smooth-skinned monsters.

Why did the ghost's shroud fall down?
Because he had no visible means of support.

What steps should you take if you're out late at night and a hungry werewolf follows you?
Very big ones.

WITCH: I'm going to Holland tomorrow.
SPOOK: Are you going by broom?
WITCH: No, by Hoovercraft.

Why are ghouls always poor?
Because a ghoul and his money are soon parted.

MRS MONSTER: We're going to the ballet tomorrow night.
MRS SPOOK: What are you going to see?
MRS MONSTER: My favourite – *Swamp Lake*.

DRACULA: Why don't you come to the Blood Ball?

SKELETON: I'm sorry, my heart's just not in it.

Why did the ghoul jump up and down?
Because he'd just swallowed his medicine but he'd forgotten to shake the bottle.

MRS MONSTER: That girl over there looks like Helen Brown.

MRS SPOOK: She looks even worse in orange.

What is big, invisible, has four wheels and flies?
The Ghost Town dustcart.

What's the different between Mozart and a corpse?
One composes and the other decomposes.

What is one hundred metres tall and goes "eef, if, of, muf"?
A backward giant.

LITTLE GHOUL: I just bought a haunted bicycle.

LITTLE GHOST: How do you know it's haunted?

LITTLE GHOUL: There are spooks in the wheels.

MONSTER: I've baked a fresh sponge cake. Try some.

PHANTOM; It's very chewy.

MONSTER: I can't believe it – I bought the sponges from Boots last night.

What happens when a giant sits on your car?
It's time to get a new car.

What's the space monster's favourite pastime?
Astronauts and crosses.

MRS SPOOK: My husband's too big. I think I'll try to shrink him.

MRS SPOOK: How will you do that?

MRS MONSTER: I'll give him condensed milk.

Which monster is the unluckiest in the world?
The Luck Less monster.

GHOUL: Dracula hit me and knocked me unconscious!

SPOOK: So you were out for the Count!

SPOOK: What is that horrible shiny green thing on your shoulders?

MONSTER: I don't know! Aaagh! Get it off!

SPOOK: Don't panic, it's only your head.

Why do vampires keep their coffins in the cellar?
Because they like to take vaulty winks.

Did you hear about the nasty slimy monster who was famous for his farmyard impressions?
He couldn't do the noises but he could *do the smells.*

SKELETON: I'm never going to dance again.
SPOOK: What happened last night then?
SKELETON: I stood in the hallway for two minutes and before I knew what had happened everyone had hung their coats on me!

MONSTER: Please marry me!
MISS GHOUL: But I can't! You've been married five times before and I've heard rumours that you killed every one of them.
MONSTER: Don't pay any attention to rumours – they're just old wives' tales.

Why did the ghosts hold a seance?
To try to contact the living.

What did Queen Victoria say when she bumped into the ghost of Charles I?
You're off your head.

How can you tell if a mummy is furious?
He flips his coffin lid.

COUNT DRACULA: I'm going to sing for you all.
MONSTER: Which song?
COUNT DRACULA: "Fangs for the Memory".

What's a vampire's favourite dance?
The fangdango.

What did everyone call Yorick when he was at school?
Numbskull.

How do monsters count to twenty-three?
On their fingers.

What do you call a skeleton who stays in bed until lunchtime?
Lazy bones.

Why wouldn't the monster play with his little brother?
He was tired of kicking him around.

Why did the monster give up boxing?
He didn't want to spoil his good looks.

Where does Count Dracula stay when he visits America?
The Vampire State Building.

What do you call two zombies tolling church bells?
Dead ringers.

Does Dr Frankenstein ever get lonely?
No, he can always make new friends.

What did the monster say to the first petrol pump he'd ever seen?
Why don't you take your finger out of your ear?

In which movie did Count Dracula make a guest appearance?
The Vampire Strikes Back.

MONSTER: I went to that Spanish restaurant you recommended.
GHOUL: What did you think of it?
MONSTER: Not much. They wouldn't serve me a Spaniard.

Which monster lives in the Royal Opera House?
The Fat Tum of the Opera.

What do you call a ten-metre-tall monster with his fingers in his ears?
Anything you like because he can't hear you.

Which monster climbs down the chimney at Christmas?
Santa Claws.

Can a toothless vampire bite you?
No, but he can give you a nasty suck.

Where are royal monsters married?
In Westmonster Abbey.

Who is the pudding monster's favourite artist?
Bottijelli.

What did the mummy say to his girlfriend?
Em-balmy about you.

What did one dragon say to the other dragon?
We really must give up smoking.

Why don't mummies catch cold?
They're always well wrapped up.

Which word describes the ghostly sight of 500 cake monsters doing the waltz?
Abundance.

Why did the headless ghost go to the psychiatrist?
Because he wasn't all there.

What kind of girl does a zombie take to the disco?
Anyone he can dig up.

Dracula's Perfect

Count Dracula runs the poshest pet shop in Ghost Town. It's by appointment to the Transylvanian aristocracy and the Bride of Frankenstein serves behind the counter! If you're ever in need of a pet, this is the place to come. Dracula can sell you a nice werewolf, guaranteed to eat anything and very fond of children, and he always has a good supply of toads and tarantulas. Step inside and take a look!

WITCH: I'd like an unusual pet, please.
DRACULA: We have just the thing. Last week we crossed a millipede with an ostrich.
WITCH: And what did you get?
DRACULA: We haven't been able to catch it yet, but when we do you can buy it!

MONSTER ASSISTANT: Your bill comes to ten pounds, Count Dracula.
DRACULA: I haven't got enough cash. I'll have to go to the blood bank.

WEREWOLF: Aaagh! I just swallowed a grand piano.
DRACULA: Are you choking?
WEREWOLF: It's true, I *did*!

hat did one werewolf say to the other?
've got a bone to pick with you.

How does Count Dracula keep fit?
He plays batminton – with real bats!

WITCH: I'd like a pet I can put in the washing machine.
DRACULA: How about a wash-and-wear-wolf?

What do werewolves write at the bottom of their thank-you letters?
Best vicious.

One morning Count Dracula arrived at the pet shop to discover that one of his werewolves was very ill, so he called the monster vet. "Thanks for coming so quickly," he said when the vet arrived. "It's this werewolf here. He simply lies on his back saying that he feels so ill he wants to die."

"Mmmmm," said the monster vet, licking his lips. "Well, you've done the right thing by sending for me!"

Why does Count Dracula go to the Earls Court exhibition centre each year?
To see the Bat Show.

MONSTER: How's the pet business, Dracula?
DRACULA: Awful! I'm nearly a hundred pints overdrawn at the blood bank.

Which of Count Dracula's pets is huge, grey and talks to itself?
A mumbo jumbo.

GHOUL: I'd like to buy some demons, please.
DRACULA: Why do you want demons?
GHOUL: You know what they say – demons are a ghoul's best friend.

What does Count Dracula feed his snakes?
Hiss fingers.

CUSTOMER: I used to be a werewolf myself.
DRACULA: Did you really?
CUSTOMER: Yes, but I'm all right noo-ooo-ooo-ooow!

How does Dracula get into his shop each morning?
He uses a skeleton key.

WITCH: That monster behind the counter at the blood bank is clean, kind, handsome, polite, helpful and efficient.
GHOUL: What a failure!

Why are Dracula's pets crazy?
Because most of them are bats.

What does Dracula call his regular customers?
His fang club.

MONSTER: Where are you going to keep your new pet snake?
ZOMBIE: Under my bed.
MONSTER: What about the smell?
ZOMBIE: It'll soon get used to it.

WITCH: I've got a complaint. This toad you sold me keeps bumping into things.

DRACULA: I expect he needs glasses.

WITCH: But I can't afford to send him to the hoptician!

Two workmen arrived at the witch's house to lay some filthy old lino on her kitchen floor. "I'm going out for a spell," she told them. "I'll leave you to it." Before long the monsters had finished their job – and jolly disgusting it looked too. There was only one problem, and that was a lump in the middle of the floor.

"Must be my sandwiches," said one monster. "I'm not going to take the lino up again." And he jumped up and down on it, trying to squash it flat. When it didn't disappear straight away, he took a big sledgehammer and bashed it again.

Just when he'd finished, the witch came back. "I found your sandwiches in the hall," she said, handing them to him. "Have you seen my pet toad? I can't find him anywhere."

DRACULA: I've just invented another new pet!
WITCH: What is it?
DRACULA: I crossed a duck and a whale . . .
WITCH: And what did you get?
DRACULA: Moby Duck!

MONSTER: I want a pet with wonderful hearing.
DRACULA: Ah, you want the eeriest!

What's huge, green and sits in the corner of Dracula's pet shop complaining?
The Incredible Sulk.

MONSTER: I want a pet that plays the banjo and menaces the bottom of the ocean.
DRACULA: Ah, you need Jaws Formby!

How do ghouls start their business letters?
Tomb it may concern . . .

How does Count Dracula stop his werewolves from howling in the back of his car?
He puts them in the front seat.

What is the best way of stopping infection from werewolf bites?
Don't bite any werewolves.

What do you call a six-foot tall pet werewolf with its fangs bared?
Sir.

WEREWOLF: Where do fleas go in winter?
VAMPIRE BAT: Search me.

WITCH: I'd like some new tiles for my bathroom.
DRACULA: But madam, this is a pet shop.
WITCH: I know – I want reptiles.

What comes with three heads, two noses and six hands?
A monster pet with spare parts.

Does Dracula stock dragons in his shop?
No, he doesn't allow smoking.

47

SHORT-SIGHTED SPOOK: I'd like to buy this creature for my pet.
DRACULA: But that's my piano!
SHORT-SIGHTED SPOOK: It has such a wonderful wide white smile!

Knock knock.
Who's there.
Dale.
Dale who?
Dale light will be the death of me!

DRACULA: This werewolf will have to go to the barber. I can't stand his hair any longer.

CUSTOMER: I can't make up my mind whether to buy a bat or a bison.
DRACULA: A bison's more useful.
CUSTOMER: Why is that?
DRACULA: You can't wash your hands in a bat.

How do fleas travel from one of Dracula's pets to another?
By itch-hiking.

DRACULA: Why do you call your pet snake Cigarette?
LITTLE MONSTER: Because I often take him outside for a drag.

Why does Dracula give lessons in bloodsucking to young vampires?
He likes to bring new blood into the business!

Have you heard what happened to the stupid werewolf? It lay down to chew a bone, and when it got up it had only three legs.

WITCH: My vulture is constipated. What should I give it?
DRACULA: I recommend chirrup of figs.

Why do people always take advantage of Count Dracula's kind heart?
Because no one gives a sucker a break.

WITCH: Your family all work in this shop, Count Dracula. You must be close.
DRACULA: We're blood relatives, and blood's thicker than water.
WITCH: So is golden syrup.

Why did the werewolf take his nose apart?
To see what made it run.

MONSTER: Which of your pets is making that strange noise in its throat?
DRACULA: That's the gargoyle.

MONSTER: Why is that werewolf covered in gold paint?
DRACULA: He has a gilt complex.

WITCH: Is that werewolf a good guard wolf?
DRACULA: No, he's a writer.
WITCH: What's his name?
DRACULA: Parker – it's his pen name.

Where do giant stingrays come from?
Stingapore.

What's black, covered in fur and can see just as well from both ends?
A werewolf wearing a blindfold.

CUSTOMER: I'd like a short vampire bat.
DRACULA: I don't recommend a short one.
CUSTOMER: Why not?
DRACULA: They're a real pain in the knee.

WITCH: I'd like a new frog, please.
DRACULA: You bought one only last week. What happened?
WITCH: It Kermit-ted suicide.

What do you call a flea that lives in a stupid werewolf's ear?
A space invader.

CUSTOMER: I'd like to buy a huge elephant with massive wings.
DRACULA: I think you want a mam-moth.

Why does Count Dracula carry a briefcase?
Because briefcases can't walk.

CUSTOMER: Why have all your werewolves got fur coats?
DRACULA: They'd look pretty silly in plastic macs!

FIRST WEREWOLF: I've got terrible acid indigestion.
SECOND WEREWOLF: Why don't you stop drinking acid?

Why does Count Dracula wear red braces?
To keep his trousers up.

Which ghost bought three bears for pets?
Ghouldilocks.

CUSTOMER: I'd like to ask a personal question, Count Dracula. Why do you always chew extra strong mints?
DRACULA: Because I suffer from bat breath.

Where can you find monster snails?
On the end of monster's fingers.

WITCH: What's blue and green, has three little red eyes and lots of hairy black legs?
DRACULA: I don't know – is it a new sort of pet?
WITCH: I'm not sure, but there's one crawling up your back.

Witch's Spell Shop

Next time you want to buy a turbo-charged broomstick or make your teacher break out in green spots, pay a visit to the Spell Shop. It's where all the witches in the Ghost Town gather to buy spells, exchange gossip and haggle over the latest magic. If you do go inside, make sure you're polite to everyone because if you aren't you might be turned into a . . .

Why do witches ride broomsticks?
Because their vacuum cleaner leads are too short.

What do you call a witch who is so nervous she can't stop shaking?
A twitch.

WITCH: Say something soft and sweet to me!
WIZARD: Mattress, sugar, bath sponge, chocolate cake . . .

Who got the higher marks in the spelling examination, the witch or the prehistoric monster?
The monster – it passed with extinction.

What do you call a witch who drives very slowly down the middle of the street?
A road hag.

What did the witch say to the zombie?
Good morning, Zombie . . .

What sort of music do witches like dancing to?
Hagtime.

What do you call a witch who goes to the beach but is too scared to go for a swim in the sea?
A chicken sandwitch.

WITCH: Please go away! You're giving me an eerie ache.
GHOST: Sorry I spook.

MONSTER: Every time we get misty weather I hear this strange croaking noise coming from your house.

WITCH: That's probably my frog horn.

What happened when the witch met the four-headed monster?

It was love at first fright.

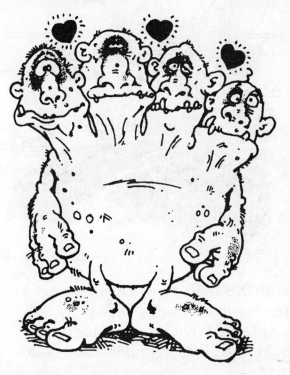

WITCH: Do you fancy a game of vampires?

SPOOK: Shall we play for money?

WITCH: Yes, for very high stakes.

Who went into the witch's house and came out alive?
The witch.

MRS MONSTER: How embarrassing! I've just met the Spellbinder twins.
MRS SPOOK: What was so embarrassing?
MRS MONSTER: I couldn't tell witch from witch.

WITCH: If a flying saucer is an aircraft, does that make a broomstick a witchcraft?

Two witches were talking about their homes. "My house is getting so ramshackle," said one. "Last night the roof sprang a leak."

"Won't your landlord come and fix it for you?" said the other.

"Fix it?" cried the other. "If I let him know he'll charge me extra rent for the use of a shower."

WITCH: Let me sit down! I just met the zombie body snatchers!
WIZARD: What happened?
WITCH: I was almost carried away!

Why did the witch stick her head into a can of yellow paint?
To see if blondes really did have more fun.

Why did the witch jump on an orange?
Because she felt like playing squash

Three witches were in the Spell Shop and having an argument about who was the best witch in the world. All of them kept talking over the top of each other. Finally one of them jumped up and yelled at the other two, "Please don't talk while I'm interrupting."

Knock, knock.
Who's there?
Ivy.
Ivy who?
Ivy cast a spell on you!

How do witches tell the time?
They use their witch watches.

What's the best way of talking to a witch?
By telephone.

Two young warlocks broke into the witch's house on Hallowe'en, when they thought she would be flying through the sky on her broomstick. But no sooner had they crept in through the window than they heard a mysterious voice. "I'm going to start by nibbling off your toes," it went. "Then I'm going to bite off your arms, and last of all I'm going to chew your head . . ."

"Aaaaagh!" cried the warlocks, getting stuck in the window frame as they both tried to squeeze out at once.

"What was that?" asked the witch, putting down her gingerbread man.

FIRST WITCH: I hear you've just come out of hospital. What did you have done?
SECOND WITCH: I had my ghoul stones removed.
FIRST WITCH: I had the same apparition!

FIRST WITCH: My boyfriend calls me Wonder Woman.
SECOND WITCH: That's because he wonders whether you're a woman or not.

Why did the wizard put birdseed in his shoes?
Because he had pigeon toes.

What do witches like to read in the newspaper?
Their horrorscopes.

FIRST WITCH: When it's wet and snowy in the winter I wear knee-high boots.
SECOND WITCH: Yes, and in spring lace-ups are the most useful sort of shoe.
FIRST WITCH: And in the summer you can't beat open-toad sandals.

WIZARD: I'm terribly sorry, but I've just cast a spell and turned your black cat into a tin of cat food. Perhaps I could replace him?
WITCH: Can you catch mice?

What are witches' favourite magazines?
The Witch Report and *Witch Broom*.

WITCH: Did you hear about the eight brainless black cats? They were called Doh, Ray, Fah, Soh, La, Ti, Doh.
MONSTER: But what about Mi?
WITCH: Sorry, I forgot about you.

What do witches' frogs sit on?
Toadstools.

Where do witches hold their parties?
In the ghost town morgue – well, you know what they say; the morgue, the merrier.

FIRST WITCH: What a beautiful coat you've got. What kind of fur is it made from?
SECOND WITCH: I don't know, but every time I walk past a werewolf the hem begins to wag at the back.

WITCH: Have you seen the newspaper headlines? Humpty Dumpty fell off the wall.
HAG: And they're not going to be able to put him back together again!
WIZARD: He wasn't what he was cracked up to be.

A witch was getting very angry because she simply could not make her fire light. She used bits of paper and straw, firflighters and everything else she could think of, but still the flames would simply flicker for a few seconds and go out. She even tried a spell that would normally set fire to things, but it wouldn't work.

Finally, just as she was getting really upset, a wizard came by. "I know what to do," he said, and he went and got a bucket of last year's coal from the bottom of the bath, put it on the fire and, abracadabra, it caught light immediately.

"How did you do that?" asked the witch amazed.

"It's easy," said the wizard. "After all, there's no fuel like an old fuel."

Every night all the little spooks and monsters of the Ghost Town go to the Spooky School where they learn useful things like how to float through walls and scare humans. Come on in and join them for a few crazy lessons!

LITTLE GHOST: I want to learn a new language so that I can talk to the two-headed Dutch monster.
GHOST TEACHER: What language does he speak?
LITTLE GHOST: Double Dutch.

GEOGRAPHY TEACHER: Where are yellow monsters found?
PUPIL: Yellow monsters are never lost.

LITTLE SPOOK: Cereal packets, crisp bags, old newspapers, cola bottles . . .
SPOOKY TEACHER: Shut up – you're talking rubbish again.

How did the little ghoul know that there was a big monster hiding under his bed?
Because when he woke up his nose was pressed against the ceiling.

Where did the class go for its Christmas outing?
The phantomime.

SPOOK FATHER: Why do you always give my son such bad marks?
SPOOK TEACHER: Because he's always making a ghoul of himself.

LITTLE SPOOK: What nationality is that new ghoul in your class?
LITTLE GHOST: Polish.
LITTLE SPOOK: How do you know?
LITTLE GHOST: Haven't you noticed how brightly he shines?

HISTORY TEACHER: Why did the Romans build straight roads?
PUPIL: Because they didn't want to drive their armies round the bend.

What happened to the little spook who slept with his head under the pillow?
The fairies pulled all his teeth out.

Where do grown-up ghosts go to study?
Ghoullege.

It was lunchtime at the spooky school and the monster teacher was supervising her class at their table. "Stop bolting your food down," she told Dr Frankenstein's monster. "And you, don't use your fingers to eat with, use a spade like I taught you."

The spooky teacher was giving some careers advice. "What do you want to be when you grow up?" she asked one ghoul.

"An air ghostess," replied the ghoul.

"And I want to be a pilot with British Scareways," said another.

WITCH: Dr Frankenstein says I'm suffering from hypnotism.
GHOST: You can't suffer from hypnotism!
WITCH: Yes I can – I've got rheumatism of the hip.

Which song is sung each day at morning assembly?
Ghoul Britannia.

SPOOK: That little skeleton stinks!
GHOUL: He won't have a bath because he's frightened he'll slip down the plughole.

A little spook got home from school and grumpily threw off his blazer and tie. "What's wrong?" asked his mother.

"We had to do lessons during the lunch hour," he complained.

"Surely not?"

"We had alphabet soup, and teacher gave us a spelling test while we ate it."

Where did the geology class go for their Christmas treat?
A rock concert.

It was lunchtime at the spooky school and every-one was eating salad. "Aaagh!" shrieked the phantom teacher. "There's a little maggot in my tomato!"

A dinner lady took the plate away. "I'm sorry," she said. "I'll go and get you a bigger one."

One pupil of the spooky school ran away with the circus. When his parents caught up with him they made him give it back.

What do spooks wear on their way to school in the rain?
Boo-ts and ghouloshes.

Who represented the spooky school at the press conference?
The spooksperson.

What happens to little monsters who think electricity is easy?
They get a nasty shock.

A little ghoul was learning to play the violin at school and used to practise each night for her parents. "Do you think I'm good?" she asked her mother.

"Yes, dear. You should be on the television."

"I'm *that* good?"

"No, but at least we could turn you off."

TEACHER: Gordon Ghoul, name three types of bird that can't fly.
GORDON GHOUL: An ostrich, a penguin, and a dead vulture.

How many letters are there in the monster alphabet?
Twenty-four – E. T. went home.

One ghost at the school is so shy that when he does his haunting practice he floats through walls backwards, goes pink, then stutters, "Excuse me . . . B-b-boo!"

What is the little ghosts' favourite TV show?
Strange Hill.

Did you hear about the Spooky School's crazy science teacher who invented a gun with three barrels?
He called it a trifle.

Why did the cross-eyed teacher leave the spooky school?
Because she couldn't control her pupils.

"Mummy, mummy, everyone at school is saying I'm a werewolf," said a pupil when he got home from the spooky school.
  "Sit down, dear, and comb your face."

How did the invisible boy upset his teachers?
He kept appearing.

SPOOKY EXAM QUESTION: If a ghost is born in Tooting, grows up in Barking, spends his life haunting in Woking and eventually dies in Peking, what is he?
ANSWER: Dead.

HISTORY TEACHER: What was the first thing that King Henry VIII did on coming to the throne?
GORDON GHOUL: He sat down.

A spook came home after his first day at school. "Who did you sit next to?" asked his mother.

"A girl monster with lovely blue hair all down her back."

"What a pity it wasn't on her head."

SPOOKY TEACHER: Which month of the year has twenty-eight days?
CLASS: They all have!

GHOST TEACHER: Where did you go for your summer holiday?
SPOOK PUPIL: Lake Eerie.

TEACHER: I want you to read this book on electricity.
LITTLE VAMPIRE: Is it *light* reading?
TEACHER: More like *current* events.

Why did the little spook stand on his head?
To turn things over in his mind.

Did you hear about the stupid monster who wanted a day off school?
He rang the teacher to tell her that he couldn't come to school because he'd lost his voice.

LITTLE GHOUL: I can't take my bike to school – it's started biting people in the street.
LITTLE MONSTER: It must be a vicious cycle.

One class of spooks were learning how to fly at supersonic speed through the air. They were very nervous, so when the first ghost had made his test flight the others crowded round. "How does it feel to hurtle through the air at two thousand kilometres an hour?" they asked.

"It hurtles!"

What happened when the pupils of the spooky school held a beauty contest?
No one won.

Why are English monsters no good at hula-hooping?
They've got stiff upper hips.

Who is the most important player in the spooky school's football team?
The ghoul keeper.

The spooky teacher was giving a lesson about monsters. "And which family does the yeti belong to?" she asked.

"I don't know," replied Gordon Ghoul. "No one in our street's got one."

GEOGRAPHY TEACHER: Which country do abominable snowmen come from?
PUPIL: Chile.

Why didn't the skeleton go to the school disco?
Because he had no body to go with.

GORDON GHOUL: The girl over there just rolled her eyes at me.
SID SPOOK: Well, roll them back before you lose them!

Why did the little ghost keep looking in the mirror?
To make sure that he wasn't still there.

Ghostly Graveyard

The ghostly graveyard is where all the ghouls and spooks gather each night. They play tag among the gravestones and love surprising any humans foolish enough to take a short cut late at night. Come and join them – tonight there's no need to be afraid!

Where do ghosts send their laundry?
To the dry screamers.

Why is the ghostly graveyard such a noisy place?
Because of all the coffin.

GHOST: I'm getting too old for this haunting business – I just don't seem to be able to frighten people any more.
GHOUL: I know, we might as well be alive for all anyone seems to care.

When do ghosts haunt tall buildings?
When they're in high spirits.

Where do ghost trains stop?
At manifest-ations.

GHOST: I went to the graveyard last night.
PHANTOM: Someone dead?
GHOST: Yes, all of them.

Why did the vicar put a fence around his graveyard?
Because everyone was dying to get in.

MRS MONSTER: What are you going to get your son for Christmas?
MRS GHOUL: I thought I'd buy him some Brute aftershave.

Two ghosts were playing in the graveyard when they saw a newcomer arrive. "You can tell he was a careful driver when he was alive," said one ghost.
"How do you know?" asked the other.
"He's wearing wing mirrors!"

Which weight do ghosts box at?
Phantom weight.

A lady was on her way home late one night and decided to save time by walking through the graveyard of her local church. She opened the gate and went in, but she had only gone a hundred metres when she heard a mysterious tapping coming from one of the graves. Nervous, but desperate to know what it was, she followed the direction the noise was coming from, until she saw a little old man chipping away at one of the gravestones. "Oh," she said with relief, "for a moment I thought I was going to see a ghost. What are you doing, carving a gravestone at midnight?"

The old man turned his pale face towards her. "When they buried me last week," he moaned, "they spelt my name wrong . . ."

How do ghouls get to work at the Monster Market each night?
On ghost trains.

SPOOK: Why are temporary teachers known as relief teachers?
GHOST: Because it's such a relief when they go.

What does the guard at the graveyard say to strangers?
Who ghosts there?

What do ghosts sing at football matches?
Here we ghost, here we ghost, here we ghost.

Where are spooky westerns set?
In Tombstone.

What games do ghosts play among the gravestones?
Haunt and seek.

Why do ghosts like tall buildings?
Because they're full of scarecases!

What did the little ghost buy from the Monster Market?
Boo-ble gum.

What's the best way to keep fit if you want to be a ghost hunter?
You must exorcise every day.

Did you hear about the most famous of all the Ghost Town phantoms?
He became spooker of the House of Commons.

What trees grow in the ghostly graveyard?
Cemetrees.

How do ghostly hens dance?
Chick to chick.

Where do phantoms go for their holidays?
The South Ghost.

GHOST: Last night I shot a monster in my pyjamas.
SPOOK: That's amazing.
GHOST: How he got into them I'll never know.

Why did the phantom from the bottom of the sea have a tap on his head?
Because he had water on the brain.

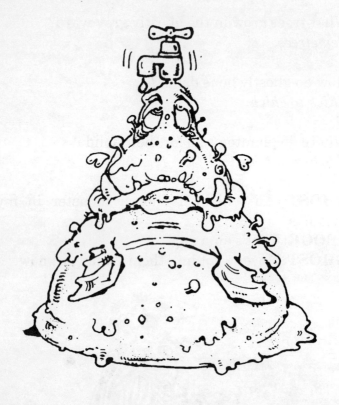

Where do ghosts stay when they go on holiday?
In ghost (guest) houses.

What do you get if you cross a ghost and a senior policeman?
A chief inspectre.

Why does Count Dracula sleep in a coffin in the ghostly graveyard?
Because he can't afford to rent a flat.

Why are old ghosts boring?
Because they're groan-ups.

A ghost sat in the graveyard one night and took out his packet of sandwiches. "Oh no, not slug and pickle," he groaned as he bit into the first, "I hate slug and pickle," and he put it aside and picked up the next sandwich in the pile.

"More slug and pickle!" he sighed as he inspected it. "They're *all* slug and pickle," he complained as he emptied his packet. "I can't eat a single one of them."

"Why don't you ask your wife to make you something else?" asked another ghost on a nearby gravestone.

"My wife doesn't make my sandwiches," sniffed the first ghost. "*I* do!"

Two spooks were having a discussion. "I've heard all your arguments, but I'm sorry," said one. "Nothing you've said can convince me that people do exist."

What did the policeman say to the three-headed ghost?
"Allo, allo, allo."

Which spook pulls ugly faces at Han Solo and Darth Vader?
Princess Leer.

What were the posh ghost's hobbies?
Haunting, shooting and fishing.

What do you call a zombie who rises from the grave after 1000 years?
Pete.

Which stall did the skeletons run at the graveyard fete?
The rattle.

What do you call a ghost underneath a car?
Jack.

SPOOK: Help! I just bumped into a human in the street!
GHOST: You need a stiff drink.
SPOOK: Yes, put some cement into my tea, will you?

Some ghosts were telling each other stories. "Have you heard about the crazy monster?" asked one. "He burst into Dr Frankenstein's surgery waving a gun and demanded that the doctor pull out all his teeth. Dr Frankenstein protested, because he said there was nothing wrong with his teeth, but the monster said that if he didn't do what he was told he'd get shot. "All right," said Dr Frankenstein. "I'll give you an injection to dull the pain."

"I don't want an injection," said the monster. "Just pull them out." Dr Frankenstein was so frightened that he'd be shot that he did as he was told. One by one, using his biggest pair of pliers, he pulled each tooth out. "When he had fnished and the monster didn't have a single tooth left, he jumped up out of the chair and pulled the trigger of the gun. A jet of water shot out and squirted Dr Frankenstein in the face. "April Fool!" yelled the monster. "I didn't really come in here to have my teeth pulled out – I just wanted a toothbrush!"

Jason's parents were about to go out for the evening, but the babysitter called to say that she wouldn't be able to come to keep an eye on him.

"Don't worry," said Jason. "I'm quite old enough to look after myself." So off his parents went.

They had only been gone a moment when the telephone rang. A creepy voice moaned down the line, "I am the phantom of Bleeding Finger, and I'll be calling at your house in one minute."

"Ha-ha," thought Jason, "it's someone playing a practical joke on me." But only a few seconds later he heard a horrible dragging noise coming up the garden path. Feeling suddenly nervous, Jason went into the kitchen and shut the door behind him. He was just in time too, because with a terrible crash the front door of the house was knocked open and something came into the hall.

Now Jason was really terrified. The thing in the hall was moaning and groaning and he could hear it dragging around, looking for him. Quickly he dashed across the kitchen and hid himself in the larder – only just in time, because the kitchen door was flung open and the monster, or whatever it was, came in rasping and creeping. For a while there was silence, apart from its heavy breathing as it searched for Jason, who was squeezed trembling and terrified in the larder. Then, suddenly, the door opened – and Jason saw before him a horrible phantom. It was green and slimy, with horrible greasy hair in patches on its head. It dragged chains behind it on the floor and, worst of all, blood trickled from one of its fingers.

"Aaaaagh!" screamed Jason. "Go away!"

"I am the phantom of Bleeding Finger," moaned the creature.

"What do you want?" cried Jason.

"Do you have a bandage you could lend me?"

Did you hear about the ghost who got stuck in a revolving door for an hour?
He didn't know whether he was coming or going.

What did the hippie monster say to the ice monster?
Real cool, man.

Did you hear about the ghost who carries his head under his arm? He went for a haircut one day, but the barber was busy. "You'll have to wait half an hour," he warned.

"That's no problem," said the ghost. "I'll leave my head here and come back for it later."

LITTLE SPOOK: Where does your sister come from?

ABOMINABLE SNOWMAN: Alaska.

LITTLE SPOOK: Don't worry, I'll ask her myself.

Why did the bald spook always sit in the graveyard?

He wanted plenty of fresh 'air!

Two lady ghosts were having a gossip in the Monster Market. "I hear you've got a job with a spiritualist," said one.

"That's right," said the other.

"And is he much good?"

"Medium, I'd say."

SPOOK: What are you burying?

GHOST: My car battery.

SPOOK: Why are you doing that?

GHOST: It's dead.

What's a ghost's last drink?

His bier.

PHANTOM: I see that Count Dracula has a new sign in the back window of his car.

SPOOK: What does it say?

PHANTOM: Please Give Blood Generously.

How many ghosts can you fit into an empty coffin?

One – after that it's not empty any more.

MONSTER: Count Dracula has asked me to oin his fang club.
GHOST: How do you do that?
MONSTER: I just have to send my name, address and blood group.

MR MONSTER: My wife has a degree in shopping.
MR GHOUL: Really?
MR MONSTER: Yes, she's studied buy-ology.

MONSTER: Give me your money or I'll batter you to death with this woven tablemat.
SPOOK: You must be a member of the Raffia!

SPOOK: I wish those skeletons would shut up.
GHOST: What instrument are they trying to play?
SPOOK: Their trom-bones.

Why is the stupid ghost like the jungle?
Both of them are thick.

What was written on the metal monster's gravestone?
Rust in Peace.

Dr Frankenstein's Surgery

Next time you have a splitting headache, go and see Dr Frankenstein for a cure. He'll prescribe you one of his special pills made half of aspirin and half of glue! As well as being the Ghost Town's favourite doctor he's also a crazy inventor. Once he crossed a raincoat with a packet of tea to produce the world's first waterproof teabag. So come on in to his waiting room and meet him yourself!

Why was Dr Frankenstein's first mechanical man so silly?
He had a screw loose.

A dragon arrived at the surgery looking very ill. "What's the matter?" asked Dr Frankenstein.

"I have a terrible stomach ache," explained the dragon.

"Have you eaten anything in the last 48 hours?"

"Only a knight in armour," said the dragon.

"And did he smell fresh when you took him out of his armour?" asked the doctor.

"You mean I was supposed to take him out of his armour?"

"Doctor, doctor," moaned the jumping monster as he crawled into the surgery, "I'm totally exhausted."

"No you're not," said Dr Frankenstein. "You're just out of bounds."

Dr Frankenstein had just performed one of his amazing operations. "I've crossed a hyena with a monster," he explained to his assistant Igor.

"And what have you got?" asked Igor.

"I don't know," replied the doctor, "but when it starts to laugh we'd better join in."

"Dr Frankenstein, Dr Frankenstein! I feel as if I'm at death's door!"

"Don't worry, I'll pull you through."

What did Dr Frankenstein's monster do when he split his sides laughing?
He ran round the town until he got a stitch in his side.

LITTLE GHOST: I think our school must be haunted by humans.
LITTLE SPOOK: How do you know that?
LITTLE GHOST: The headmaster's always going on about the school spirit.

DR FRANKENSTEIN: I've had a great idea for a new monster! I'm going to cross a four-wheel drive vehicle with a dog.
IGOR: What will that make?
DR FRANKENSTEIN: A Land Rover.

A monster walked into Dr Frankenstein's waiting room and sat down on a chair. After a couple of minutes he slipped off the chair and began rolling around on the floor, bumping into other patients and knocking over the umbrella stand and the table with its horror magazines. The other patients began to scream and yell.

"What's going on?" asked Dr Frankenstein, emerging from his surgery.

"I'm sorry, doctor," gasped the patient as he rolled around on the floor. "It's just that I feel like a snooker ball."

"In that case," said Dr Frankenstein, "come to the front of the cue."

DR FRANKENSTEIN: How did you burn your ear like this?

STUPID MONSTER: I tried to listen to a match.

FRANKENSTEIN'S MONSTER: Well, what does my brain X-ray show?

DR FRANKENSTEIN: Nothing.

"Doctor, doctor, can you help me out?"
  "Which way did you come in?"

NURSE: Dr Frankenstein, there's a ghost waiting out here to see you.

DR FRANKENSTEIN: Tell him I can't see him.

FRANKENSTEIN'S MONSTER: Dr F's made me a girlfriend.
NURSE: Is she nice?
FRANKENSTEIN'S MONSTER: She's very shy. She even goes into a cupboard to change her mind.

DR FRANKENSTEIN: Your suit fits you like a bandage!
MUMMY: Yes, I got it by accident. . . .

"Doctor, doctor, I'm worried about my son. I know monsters are supposed to be big, but he's thirty metres tall and weighs three hundred tonnes."

"Don't worry, he'll grow out of it."

DR FRANKENSTEIN: I think I'll go down to the gymnasium this morning.
NURSE: Why?
DR FRANKENSTEIN: I feel like a bit of body building.

DR FRANKENSTEIN: When is my lunch going to be ready?
MONSTER COOK: Be patient – I've only got four pairs of hands.

MRS GHOST: Doctor, I'm so worried about my baby!
DR FRANKENSTEIN: Does he keep screaming?
MRS GHOST: No, he's in such good spirits!

GHOST: Did you enjoy the horror movie last night?
DR FRANKENSTEIN: No, it was the usual boring story. Man meets woman, man loses woman, man makes another woman.

MRS MONSTER: It's my old mum, Dr Frankenstein. I can't look after her any more.
DR FRANKENSTEIN: I'll put you in touch with the Old Folks Gnome.

A monster raced into Dr Frankenstein's surgery. "Doctor, doctor, how long can someone survive without a brain?"

"I don't know. How old are you?"

GHOST: Can you help me, Dr Frankenstein?
DR FRANKENSTEIN: You really need to see a surgical spirit.

Why did the skeleton go to see Dr Frankenstein?
Because he didn't have any guts.

"Doctor, doctor, my werewolf just swallowed a machine gun!"

"For goodness sake don't point him at me!"

94

"Doctor, doctor, can you give me something for my liver?"

"How about some bacon and onions?"

FRANKENSTEIN'S MONSTER: I want to change my mind.
DR FRANKENSTEIN: I'll make sure the new one works better than the old one did.

DR FRANKENSTEIN: Why didn't you call me sooner? Your wife is very sick!
MR MONSTER: I know, but I wanted to give her a chance to get better first.

A balding monster came to see Dr Frankenstein. "Can you give me a hair transplant?"

"No," said the doctor, "but I could try shrinking your head to fit what you've got left."

Sad news. Dr Frankenstein raced out to save a monster who'd got stuck in a barrel of beer, but he arrived too late.

"Is he dead?" asked another monster.

"Yes," said Dr Frankenstein, "he came to a bitter end."

MONSTER MANIA

A word from Dr Frankenstein

Let me introduce myself. I am Dr Frankenstein, the *great* Dr Frankenstein, the man
who created the most remarkable monster the
world has ever known. Frankenstein's
Monster!

Since I made my monster, many other monsters have been created. Monsters living in
the ocean depths, monsters prowling from
graves at night, monsters that looked like men
during the day but which turned into ghastly
creatures of the night as soon as the sun had
set, all of these have plagued the earth at one
time or another.

But my own monster was different from all
of these. It was the product of the mind of a
genius. It was the result of scientific study.
Had it worked as I intended it would have
been one of the most remarkable scientific
discoveries ever made, perhaps the most
remarkable . . . the discovery of life itself! But
as we all know my monster was only a partial
success, and after a certain amount of incon-

venience I had to return to my drawing board to try again.

While I was sitting in the windmill that I had built to replace the old one, which was burned down when the angry villagers destroyed my monster and the laboratory in which it was hiding, I had an idea. Why should other people not share the thrill that I feel whenever I am in the presence of monsters? Why should they not be allowed to taste some of the mysteries of the forbidden world in which I have become so famous.

In the pages that follow, there are games to play when your monster friends call round to see you. There are jokes and riddles to keep them amused. There are ways that you can make them feel more at home by making yourself look like a monster, and there are ideas for developing and enlarging your own knowledge of monsters. Have fun learning about monsters, and you never know, one day you may find yourself trying to make a monster almost as good as mine.

'Happy horror'! Or should I say 'Good ghouling'?!

Frankenstein and friends

A who's who of horror

You will probably know the names of most of the characters described in the next few pages, but you may not know their stories, what they did and why they are famous.

The Bride of Frankenstein

Frankenstein's bride is not the intended wife of the mad doctor who created the monster, she was the intended wife of the monster itself. In fact, the film *Bride of Frankenstein*, made in 1935 as a sequel to Frankenstein, was directly responsible for the error which is now commonly made, that Frankenstein is the name of the monster.

After Dr Frankenstein had created his homemade man and successfully brought him to life, he was visited by his old university professor, Dr Praetorius.

The professor had been experimenting with making living people too. But his results were only miniature men and women. Unlike his pupil, though, Dr Praetorius had grown his living creatures like plants. He had grown them from tiny cultures. When he saw the success that his pupil had achieved with his huge monster, Dr Praetorius suggested that they should try to provide the monster with a mate, so that together they could create a new civilisation of specially bred men and women.

Dr Frankenstein was reluctant to begin with, but after the monster was persuaded by Dr Praetorius to kidnap Frankenstein's wife he agreed to join in the project.

He and Dr Praetorius took the remains of Madeleine Ernestine, who had died when she was nineteen. After performing the necessary operations on her, they placed her bandaged body under an electric Cosmic Diffuser and brought her to life.

However, the monster's intended bride took one look at her future husband and was disgusted at the idea of marrying anything so ugly.

Hurt by her rejection, the monster allowed his master and his wife to escape before blowing up the laboratory, the evil Dr Praetorius and his wife-to-be.

Dr Caligario

Dr Caligari was a wandering showman who used to entertain crowds at fairgrounds. His particular show consisted of a black-clothed figure called Cesare which he kept in a coffin, and which he woke during the performances to tell fortunes to the spectators.

Each time he woke him up Dr Caligari claimed that Cesare had slept for twenty years, and the eerie sight of the figure waking in the coffin convinced the crowd that he was telling the truth.

They also believed Dr Caligari when he told them that Cesare knew all that there was to know in the future. For whenever someone in the audience asked how long he was going to live and Cesare told him that he would die soon, that person did indeed die.

The reason for this was quite simple. Every night after the show, Cesare left his coffin and murdered whoever had asked the question. Cesare killed at Dr Caligari's command because the doctor controlled his mind.

In the end though the doctor was found out, and it was discovered that he was in fact none other than the director of the neighbouring lunatic asylum. He had somehow gained power over the minds of the living dead, and of course was as mad as a hatter himself.

Dr Jekyll and Mr Hyde

Dr Jekyll and Mr Hyde were one and the same man.

As a young man, Dr Jekyll had been wild and carefree, and when he grew older he became fascinated with the idea of separating the evil parts of a man's nature from the good and virtuous parts.

He began to make scientific experiments to see if it was possible to make this transformation and in the end he discovered a secret potion which would indeed produce two separate beings.

The evil-looking, evil-doing half of his personality appeared in the form of Mr Hyde, while the good half was Dr Jekyll.

To begin with Mr Hyde only made a few brief appearances in public, but even these were enough to show his brutal, savage nature. In spite of Hyde's behaviour in public, Dr Jekyll still maintained that he could control him. But soon Mr Hyde began to take over the doctor and one awful morning Dr Jekyll woke up to find Mr Hyde's hand on the sheet, which showed that he had lost control of his experiment – he was living inside Mr Hyde's body.

The doctor managed to obtain a special medicine which changed him back into his correct form, but gradually the effect of the medicine wore off and it became impossible for Mr Hyde to change back into Dr Jekyll. He hid himself away behind a locked door, passing notes underneath to his butler. But when two friends finally broke down the door they found him dead. That is they found Mr Hyde dead in Dr Jekyll's clothes. One man had killed the other or both had committed suicide. Who was to say?

Dr Jekyll and Mr Hyde were invented by Robert Louis Stevenson in his short novel *The Strange Case of Dr Jekyll and Mr Hyde*, published in 1886. It is on this book that the many film versions of the story are based. (It is probably the most frequently filmed horror story of all.) Two famous versions are the 1920 silent one, starring John Barrymore, and the 1931 sound movie, starring Fredric March. A recent television adaptation starred David Hemmings in the title roles.

Dr Moreau

Dr Moreau was another mad scientist who became obsessed with the idea of improving human life through the use of animals. In his case however he tried to turn animals into humans, with horrifying results!

By turning the animals of the jungle into human shapes and giving them the power of speech, Dr Moreau attempted to parallel the achievements of Nature. He tried to create his own species of creatures independently from the natural processes of evolution.

The creatures he produced lived wretched, painful lives as neither men nor beasts. He developed a Leopard Man, a creature that was a cross between a goat and an ape, and a number of creatures similar to wolves.

In the end however the pitiful creatures began to revert to their animal state and they turned against the evil man who had tried to change them. Dr Moreau perished on his accursed island and the wicked plan which he had tried to develop perished with him.

Dr Moreau was created by H. G. Wells, famous for his novels which looked into the future, in *The Island of Dr Moreau*.

Dracula

Count Dracula was the most famous of the vampires. He lived in the fifteenth century in an ancient crumbling castle in Transylvania, which is now part of modern Romania.

He was not alone in the castle however, for with him lived a group of female vampires. Together they terrorised the surrounding countryside, stealing children and killing local men and women so that they could drink their blood.

The evil Count was not content to limit his wicked practices to Transylvania however, for he bought an old abbey in England which he planned to use as his base for spreading vampirism in this country.

After he had bought the property, Dracula was visited by an Englishman called Jonathan Harker. He was a lawyer who was concerned with the purchase of the abbey. Harker arrived in Transylvania only to be warned by the local people that it would be dangerous for him to proceed to Dracula's castle. However, he completed his journey through dark forests filled with wolves and arrived at the ghostly castle, to be met by the inhuman Count himself.

At first Harker did not suspect that Dracula was a vampire. But after a few days he began to realise that there was something strange about his host. The Count appeared in his room one morning while he was shaving, but although the mirror that Harker was using showed everything else in the room, there was no reflection of the Count!

Then he woke up one morning to find himself surrounded by three strange women. One tried to bite his neck, but Dracula came in just in time and told the women to leave Harker alone. He gave them a sack with a small bundle inside for their supper, and from inside the sack the bundle cried like a human being!

In the end Dracula made Harker a prisoner in his castle and left for England himself. On the sea-crossing the Count killed all the ship's crew to drink their blood, and when he arrived in England he attacked a woman called Lucy Westenra. She died as a result of his attack, but rose from the dead as a vampire herself and terrorised London, just as Dracula had terrorised Transylvania.

Fortunately a Dutch expert in dealing with vampires, Dr van Helsing, succeeded in driving a wooden stake into Lucy's heart, which was the only way of killing a vampire.

Meanwhile Dracula attacked Jonathan Harker's wife, and then fled back to Transylvania. Harker managed to escape from the castle and he and Dr van Helsing pursued the Count back to his castle, where in the end they managed to stab a knife deep into his heart, so bringing to an end the deadly career of the most famous vampire of them all.

Dracula's story was immortalised in a novel by Bram Stoker at the end of the nineteenth century, and most of the Dracula films are broadly based on this book. However, it is not thought that Stoker invented the character; he had heard stories about the evil Count, including the one about Vlad the Impaler (see p. 200).

Frankenstein

Strictly speaking the most famous of all monsters should be called Frankenstein's monster, because it was created by Dr Frankenstein. However, it has become so well-known as Frankenstein, that is what we are calling it here.

Frankenstein's appearance is certainly the most

frightening of all the monsters'. He was created from pieces of several dead bodies. Dr Frankenstein wanted to make a super-human creature, so he chose limbs and organs from the largest corpses, taking them from newly-made graves and from gallows where they were still hanging.

The result was a ghastly-looking creature with a square skull, a huge scar on its forehead and electrodes on either side of its throat. After stitching together the gory limbs, the doctor wrapped his monster in bandages and then hoisted it to the roof where it could be struck by lightning. The electric force of a sudden bolt of lightning brought the monster to life. The gruesome experiment had succeeded.

However, after this first success things started to go wrong. The monster killed the doctor's hunch-backed assistant, Fritz, and later killed his former teacher, Van Sloan. Then it escaped and terrorised the surrounding countryside, where it killed peasants and even tried to take away the doctor's fiancée.

Eventually the monster was cornered by a crowd of villagers carrying torches. They forced it back into the old windmill which the doctor had used as his laboratory and burnt the windmill and the monster to the ground. At least that is what the villagers thought: but the monster escaped from the burning mill unnoticed and disappeared, to terrorise the world once more!

The story of Frankenstein was originally written by Mary Shelley, the poet's wife, when she was a young girl of nineteen. It was published as a book in 1816 and since then countless stage and screen versions have been produced, including the classic 1931 film starring Boris Karloff as the monster.

Godzilla

Godzilla was a gigantic prehistoric lizard, which lived undisturbed for thousands, perhaps millions of years, deep down in the Pacific Ocean. It looked like a cross between a dragon and a fearsome prehistoric animal called *tyrannosaurus rex*. He first appeared to modern audiences in a Japanese film, *Gojira*, made in 1954.

Every year the natives of a small Pacific island had sent a gift to the monster to ensure that it did not do them any harm. The gift was always a girl set adrift on a raft, for that was the only present that would guarantee peace for the islanders. They and their ancestors had been paying this human sacrifice for centuries until one year there was an atomic test explosion in the ocean where the monster lived.

The one hundred and thirty metre high monster was infuriated by this disturbance of its home waters. It rose out of the deep and made its way towards Japan, breathing fire like all the best dragons. But Godzilla's fire was different: it was radioactive.

Godzilla attacked the Japanese capital Tokyo. It crushed skyscrapers like matchboxes and ate trains like sticks of liquorice. In the end it virtually destroyed the huge city.

There was only one way of destroying the monster, but the consequences of carrying it out were almost as disastrous as the damage caused by the monster. Finally, however, the decision was taken to proceed with this daring plan.

A famous Japanese scientist, Dr Seriza, destroyed all the oxygen in the ocean. This killed Godzilla, but it also killed all the other creatures in the sea.

When Dr Seriza realised what he had done and what the awful consequences were, the guilt was more than he could bear, and he committed *hara-kiri*, which meant killing himself according to a time-honoured Japanese ritual.

Golem

The golem has been connected with the Jewish faith since the time of the great Jewish book the Talmud. In this book of Jewish law *golem* is the word used to describe Adam's body before God gave it life? and the word has come to mean a body without a soul.

Traditionally the golem was a monster made of clay that looked like a human being and which could be brought to life by magic power.

The magic power is stored in a word which the golem carries written on a charm hanging round its neck. This word is *emeth*, which means truth. When the golem is brought to life wearing this charm it behaves rather like a zombie. It cannot speak, but it is able to understand and obey the commands of its master.

Like all the best monsters though, the golem has one big drawback. It grows bigger and stronger every day until even its master becomes afraid of it. When this happens the master has to remove the charm from the golem or rub out the first letter of the magic word to make it read *meth*. *Meth* means *he* is *dead* and changing the word to this has the same effect as removing the charm. The life is taken from the monster and it returns to being a model of lifeless clay.

One very famous golem is said to have been made in the Middle Ages by the Jews who lived in Prague, the capital of Czechoslovakia. The Jews there were threatened with persecution and one of their religious leaders, a rabbi, made a golem according to an ancient custom he had discovered. The monster was brought to life and helped to protect the community from persecution.

The Hunchback of Notre Dame

The hunchback was a hideously deformed creature that lived in the Middle Ages. A hunchback is a person with a deformed spine which causes an ugly hump on his back. But this hunchback, called Quasimodo, had more than a hump to make him look repulsive. He had a huge wart that covered his left eye, his breastbone stuck out, his head was squashed between his shoulders and he had bowed legs. His story was first told by Victor Hugo in his novel *Notre Dame de Paris* written in 1831.

Quasimodo was discovered by a young priest at the great cathedral in Paris called *Notre Dame*. He was only a child then but his appearance was so horrible that he was teased and tormented for being half-human. However, the priest took compassion on him and looked after him in the cathedral. When he was fourteen a further tragedy hit the hunchback: the tremendous noise of the great cathedral bells burst his eardrums and made him deaf. He was thus even more cut off from other people, and by a cruel quirk of fate the only sound he could hear was the ringing of the bells which had deafened him.

Throughout his life Quasimodo was persecuted and tormented because of his deafness and his deformity. No one showed any sympathy for him apart from the priest who first befriended him, until one day, after a brutal flogging and stoning, he cried for a drink of water. Nobody offered him a drink. The crowd stood jeering and unmoved, when slowly, one figure came out from the crowd, and a beautiful gypsy girl called Esmeralda went to the wretched cripple and offered him a gourd of water to drink.

Quasimodo fell in love with her at first sight, and later he had a chance to rescue her from the executioner and hide her in his lair, high up in the bell tower of the great cathedral.

If you think that the story reminds you of the famous story of Beauty and the Beast, you would be right!

Over the years many actors have played the part of the deformed dwarf. In 1923 Lon Chaney starred in a classic silent film *The Hunchback of Notre Dame* and another well-known version was made in 1939 with Charles Laughton as the hunchback.

King Kong

King Kong probably needs no introduction. He is foremost among the great monsters of the world of horror. Most people know that King Kong was a giant ape nearly twenty metres high, but for many their knowledge ends there. In fact he was a monster specially created for a film made in 1932–3.

King Kong lived on a remote island somewhere in the South Seas. The island had the gruesome name of Skull Island and understandably very few men had ever been there. However, an American film crew decided to visit the island to see if there was any truth in an ancient Malay legend about a monstrous, all-powerful creature whose reign kept the island in constant fear.

Among the film party was an actress called Ann Darrow. She was spotted by the witch king of the island who decided that she would make a suitable gift to the island's terrible monster. So the actress was captured and offered to the monster.

King Kong came stomping out of the jungle and eagerly snatched his present. Then he carried her away deep into the jungle.

He was pursued, however, and was eventually overcome by gas and captured by the film party. The actress was freed and they all sailed back to America, bringing with them the monster, bound in chains.

Once in New York, King Kong was put on display and proved to be a very popular attraction.

However, he managed to escape, causing chaos in the city. King Kong destroyed buildings and trains and finally climbed to the top of the tallest building in New York, the Empire State Building, where he made his final stand before being shot down by fighter planes.

The Mummy

In ancient Egypt there was a tradition of preserving the bodies of famous men and women after they had died. Their bodies were treated with special ointments and wrapped in long pieces of cloth before being laid to rest in their coffins. And in this preserved state they have become known as mummies.

The famous horror monster called the Mummy was one of these ancient Egyptian corpses; it first appeared in a 1932 Hollywood film starring Boris Karloff. Three thousand years ago it had lived as a prince called Kharis. Kharis had loved a princess called Anaka, but Anaka died young and in his grief Kharis had defied the gods and tried to bring her back to life.

In order to do this he had stolen the secret of Eternal Life from the temple of the goddess Isis. But the goddess had warned the temple guards, who caught Kharis red-handed and he was punished by having his tongue torn out and being buried alive.

After three thousand years an archaeological expedition succeeded in breaking into the tomb of Kharis's dead love, princess Anaka, and took the mummy, which had been the princess, back with them to America.

However, their action had been seen by the guardian of the ancient rites. He had been steadily feeding the mummy of Kharis with the secret fluid made from tana leaves. The fluid made from three leaves was enough to keep the mummy alive, but when the guardian increased the dose to the fluid of nine leaves the mummy was revived and given incredible strength.

Brought to life once again, Kharis set off to save his dead love. The mummy travelled to America where it found the archaeologist who had stolen Anaka's mummy. There he killed all those involved in the theft before finally perishing in a fire himself.

The Phantom of the Opera

Like the Hunchback of Notre Dame, the Phantom of the Opera lurked in one of the most famous buildings in Paris, the French capital; this time in the Opera House. He was created by a novelist called Gaston Laroux whose story *The Phantom of the Opera* was published in 1908. However, this monster is most familiar as portrayed in the famous 1925 film which is based on the book.

The phantom dwelt in the maze of passages and cellars that lay beneath the great theatre. It was sometimes seen scurrying away into a dark corner, but its voice was heard everywhere, because in its lifetime it had been a famous ventriloquist called Erik.

The phantom had had its own way in the Opera House for many years until two new managers took over the running of it. They did not pay any attention to the rumours and stories about the phantom to begin with. When they were asked for 240,000 francs every year and for box number five to be reserved for the phantom permanently, they thought that someone was playing a joke on them. Then things started to go wrong.

One of the leading singers suddenly lost her voice in the middle of a performance. During another performance, a huge chandelier mysteriously crashed into the auditorium, killing one of the audience. And then one by one people began to disappear, or were found dead under strange circumstances.

At the same time the phantom had fallen in love with a young singer, and it used its own musical powers to inspire her to sing brilliantly when she was called on to take over from one of the stars at very short notice. As in all the best horror stories, though, the heroine was loved by a handsome hero, and when the phantom realised it had a rival, it kidnapped the singer and kept her in its lair deep down in the cellars.

During her captivity the singer snatched off the

phantom's mask to reveal a hideous death-mask of a face. But in the end the singer showed pity for the phantom, and it agreed to release her, before it was finally exorcised from the Opera House. Once more beauty had conquered the beast!

The Reptile

Of all the animal species, reptiles are the ones we usually find most repulsive. Snakes, lizards, toads and other slithery creatures seldom fail to send shivers down our spines. So the combination of a beautiful woman and a horrible venomous snake is certain to make our flesh creep – and that is just what the Reptile did.

The Reptile had the body of a woman but the head of a snake. It fed on living animals but it preferred to eat human beings.

Originally the Reptile had been an English girl living in India. Even though the British had been in control of India for a hundred years, there were still many mysterious traditions and secret groups that existed and over which the British had no control. These oriental sects, as the groups were called, practised many strange customs and ancient rites which were protected from outsiders by terrible curses.

This particular English girl had become fasci-

119

nated by the activities of one of the sects that had come originally from Burma. However, she had pried too closely into their activities and had fallen under their particular curse. She was made to spend the rest of her life as part woman, part snake.

Her secret was only discovered by a young man who happened to visit her house, where she lived with her father. He noticed that the house was strangely warm and stuffy. But his fears were confirmed that night when he was attacked by an awful monster which was half snake, half woman. The attack failed and the following day the visitor found the young woman lying in the cellar next to a sulphur pit eating rats and mice.

The visitor escaped from the horror before his eyes, but the Reptile lived on to kill even her own father before being finally destroyed by fire.

Vampires

Vampires are legendary creatures which for centuries have been part of the folklore of different countries throughout the world. They are living corpses which have returned from the grave to haunt men and women. Although few people believe in vampires today the legends surrounding them still survive.

Traditiohally vampires left their graves at night

to walk out and suck blood from their victims. Human blood was the food which kept vampires alive and they sucked this either from living people or from the corpses of those who had recently died.

In many countries vampires were thought to have been people who met violent deaths. Criminals and people who had committed suicide were always popular candidates for vampirism. But the fresh blood which they sucked through sharp fangs from their victims' necks prevented the vampires' bodies from rotting away, so that they were free to haunt those whom they had known during their lives. And there are many accounts of vampires' coffins, opened many months after their death, and found to contain bodies which looked as if they were asleep, and not dead at all.

Vampires attacked their victims at night under the cover of darkness. They also had the power to hypnotise their victims during an attack, which meant that the victims never remembered the fangs puncturing their necks or the blood being sucked from their bodies. This hypnotic power also allowed vampires to attack the same victims several times before draining them completely of blood.

Vampires were not only considered to be dangerous and evil themselves; they were also believed to spread plagues and, worse still, they were thought to make their victims vampires too.

So over the centuries many measures were taken to protect both the living and the dead from these terrible creatures. Plants like wild roses and garlic were said to ward off vampires; so were crosses and fire. Great care was taken with the burial of corpses that were in danger of becoming vampires. These were often buried with flowers and garlic. Sometimes they were buried at cross-roads so that if the corpse did become a vampire it would not be able to find its way back to torment its relatives and friends. But in spite of these careful measures, vampires did sometimes appear and then there were special ways of dealing with them.

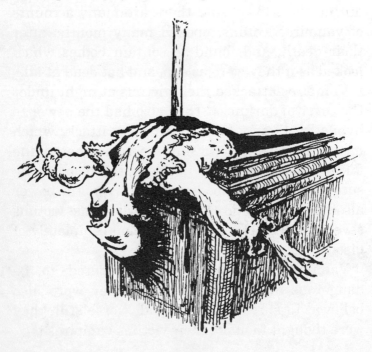

The most common method of killing a vampire once and for all was to drive a stake through its heart with one blow. Sometimes red hot nails were used instead of a stake. Other methods included boiling the vampire's heart in oil, or cutting off its head with a gravedigger's spade.

Once the vampire had been effectively killed it had to be buried in a special way. Here again there were different ways of doing this. In some countries vampires' graves were covered with heavy stones to make sure that they could not climb out. Elsewhere vampires were buried with garlic in their mouths, willow wood crosses under their arms, and wild flowers scattered in the coffin, just to make sure that their souls finally found rest.

But if, like a lot of people, you think that all this talk about vampires is just a lot of superstitious mumbo-jumbo which no one in their right mind could possibly believe today, bear in mind that, as recently as 1969, villagers in Romania, a country with a long tradition of vampires, took steps to make sure that one corpse in their village did not become a vampire – they even drove a stake through its heart!

Werewolves

The name 'werewolf' comes from two Anglo-Saxon words: *wer*, meaning a man, and *wulf*, meaning a wolf. So a werewolf came to mean a man or woman who could change into a wolf. Like vampires, werewolves are part of folklore, but they have been taken over by the film industry. One of the most famous werewolf movies, *The Wolf Man*, was made in 1941 and starred Lon Chaney Jr.

Werewolves have always been considered evil. They were believed to prowl at night in search of lonely travellers, whom they attacked and killed in order to eat their flesh and drink their blood. In this respect werewolves were thought to be very like vampires and it was often believed that they became vampires after death unless the necessary steps were taken to prevent this happening.

Some werewolves were said to be half man and half wolf, while others apparently turned their skin inside out when they appeared in public as ordinary people.

Some men became werewolves after being cursed by an evil charm. Others became werewolves after eating the flesh of something killed by a wolf, or after drinking water that had collected in a wolf's footprint.

The sharp-eyed observer could usually detect

signs of a werewolf in another's appearance. People who were unusually hairy with straight, bushy eyebrows and short pointed ears were prime suspects, and if their third fingers were as long as their second fingers, and there was hair on the palms of their hands, they were as good as convicted.

Once a werewolf had been wounded, it returned to its human form, and this usually helped to identify it, since it could be traced by the trail of blood left behind. Once it had been discovered however, the only sure way of killing the beast was to shoot it with a bullet made from the silver of a crucifix, or to stab it with a dagger made from the same metal.

Zombies

For over three hundred years the natives of the islands in the West Indies, particularly Haiti, have lived in fear of the walking dead, which they call zombies. These creatures have been taken from their graves shortly after burial by the evil power of a magician. Under this power they obey his commands as silent, living corpses.

Traditionally, magicians – voodoo priests – used magic powers to raise zombies from their graves, but in all probability they used poisonous drugs which made the zombie appear to be dead in the first place. Then after burial had taken place, the magician stole the body from the grave and revived it with more drugs. So in reality the zombie had never died. It had merely been kept in a state that seemed like death. Once restored, though, the magician had to keep the zombie in a hypnotic state to ensure that it obeyed his commands and could not rebel against him. So it lived like an animated corpse, looking at the world through deathly glazed eyes and shuffling through life in ragged clothes under its master's constant control.

Strangely enough, the only way in which a zombie could be freed from this state was by eating salt and, since salt is very easy to come by, every zombie master must have lived in peril of his zombie work-force suddenly tasting salt and either dying, or worse still, turning on him to gain their revenge.

Ghoulish giggles

Why did Frankenstein give up boxing?
Because he did not want to spoil his looks.

What does a well-mannered vampire say?
Fang you very much.

How many monsters can fit into an empty tele-phone box?
One. After that it's no longer empty, is it?

Which famous monster was also the President of France?
Charles de Ghoul.

Where does a vampire save his money?
At a blood bank.

What sort of horse does the headless horseman ride?
A nightmare.

Which ballet do monsters like best?
Swamp Lake!

What makes cemeteries very noisy?
The coffin.

Do you know what wears a black cape, flies around at night and sucks people's blood?
Of course you do. A mosquito with a black cape.

What game does Dr Jekyll enjoy playing?
Hyde and seek.

How does a monster count to twenty-three?
On its fingers.

Do monsters really do all the frightening and terrible things you see in films?
No. They use stunt men.

The look of Frankenstein

How to turn yourself into a monster!

Here are some ideas for ways to dress up and make yourself look like some of the most fiendishly frightening monsters of all time.

Guardian of the tomb

The guardian of the tomb is a ghastly-looking skeleton with a frightening skull. If you can find an old sheet (*do* ask a grown-up first) then you can make a shroud which will cover all of your body and leave only the skull showing.

To make-up as the guardian skeleton you will need: cold cream; white face powder or white stage foundation; black eyeliner; and tissues.

To begin with, gather all your hair away from your face and forehead, and rub cold cream onto your face (this makes it easier to take off the make-up when you have finished).

Using a powder puff or a piece of cotton wool,

powder your face white, or rub on white foundation, *but* do not put it round your eyes and nose;
leave these for the eyeliner. Do make your lips a
ghostly white, though.

Use the black eyeliner to paint large black
circles round your eyes. Here again ask Mum or
your sister to show you how she uses eyeliner,
because you have to be careful not to get it in your
eyes.

When you have made matching circles round
each eye, paint your nose black with the eyeliner
too. Try to make it a filled-in U-shape, so it looks
like a hollow in the bone of the 'skull'.

The next thing to do is to paint your cheeks.
Start with your eyeliner level with the middle of
your ear. Draw it along your cheek bone until it is
about four centimetres from your nose, then curve
it down to pass about two centimetres away from
the corner of your mouth. Take the line down to
your jaw and under the chin. Draw a similar line
on the other cheek and fill in the areas with the
black eyeliner.

Now draw three lines across from one black
cheek to the other. The first line passes through
your sealed lips. The second line passes between
this and your nose. And the third line passes
between the middle line and your chin. These are
the lines used to mark the teeth in the skull.

Paint one row of teeth above your mouth and
the other below, so that when you open your

mouth two ghastly jaws will open. If you paint one or two teeth black, they will look even more frightening.

The last lines are wavy lines to make the skull look old and cracked. One line runs along the forehead. One line runs under each eye and a line like an upside-down T joins the two circles round the eyes. Two lines run from the outside of the eye circles to the edge of the black cheeks and another two run from the middle of these lines up to the forehead.

Once you have made-up your face, put on the sheet – and you will be ready to scare the living daylights out of all your friends!

To prepare the sheet, fold it in half and cut half an egg-shaped piece out of the middle to make an oval hole, a little smaller than your face. Sew the sides of the sheet together, making sure to leave room for your hands, and then put it over your head, fitting the oval round your face, so that the sheet covers your hair and tucks under your chin.

If you are able to dye the sheet black the effect will be very scary!

Then you will be ready to haunt the world and terrorize all who dare to visit the tomb.

Wolfman

The wolfman only appears at the time of a full moon, but when he does come out he is one of the most awful-looking monsters that walk the earth. (With a little imagination there is no reason why you should not be a wolfwoman too. She could be just as frightening!)

To make-up as a wolfman you will need: eyeliner that is the same colour as your own hair; cotton wool; spirit gum; cold cream; and cheese wax or white plasticine.

To begin with brush your hair back from your forehead, holding it back with a hair grip if necessary. Then rub a little cold cream in your palms and rub it into your face; it will make it easier to take off the make-up when you have finished.

Now you are ready to begin the terrifying change from the smiling face in the mirror to the ghastly, hairy beast that comes out with the full moon.

Paint your face with the eyeliner, making sure that none of it gets into your eyes, and leaving your chin white. Be sure, too, that you leave some stripes of skin unpainted. These should reach out like sunbeams from the bridge of your nose across your cheeks and forehead, and from the corners of your mouth. They are the lines along which you will attach the hair.

Start to stick the 'hair' to your face near the corners of your mouth. Take a few strips of cotton wool and dip the end in the spirit gum. Place the first piece at the corner of your mouth hanging down. The second piece goes above this and so on up the sides of your nose to your cheek bones.

Again *do* make sure that you *only* use a gum which is safe to use on your skin. If you are in doubt, ask at a large chemist's shop, or at any shop which sells theatrical make-up.

Work on your chin next. Stick some pieces of cotton wool on the bottom of your chin. Then stick a few more just below your mouth. This wool should be quite thick, so that the 'hair' completely covers the skin on your chin.

Now you work on the top of your head. For this you will need to cut, or pull out strands of cotton wool about forty centimetres long. You will need about a dozen of these long strands. Stick them to your forehead pointing up, so that they fall backwards over your own hair.

To complete the 'hair' glue one long piece in the middle of your forehead sticking up over your head, and carefully stick several short bushy pieces over your eyebrows.

Once you have finished the sticking, use a pair of scissors to trim the bottom and sides of your 'beard'. Streak the cotton wool, using a little eyeliner.

Finally add the teeth. These are made from rolling and shaping the cheese wax or plasticine.

When the wax is soft shape two pieces like a dog's fangs and stick them to the third tooth from the centre on your bottom jaw. Make sure that your own teeth are completely dry, though, before you stick on the wax: if they are still moist, the wax will not stay there.

To remove the make-up, use cold cream and water. Moisten the cotton wool before you pull it off. It hurts if you try to take it off dry. Then rub your face with the cream to take off the eyeliner, and finally wash with soap and water.

Do-it-yourself Dracula

The Dracula make-up is one of the simplest to do, but you really need a Dracula costume to go with it to get the best horror effect.

For the make-up you will need: white eyeshadow or white stage make-up, or white powder; black eyeliner; grey eyeshadow; cold cream; and cheese wax or white plasticine.

In all the pictures of Dracula that you have ever seen his hair has always been brushed straight back from his forehead, hasn't it? So you must start by making yours look the same. You might need to use some hair lotion to hold it in place. If you do, make sure that you do not get any in your eyes. An alternative is to damp your hair with water.

Rub your face with cold cream, then cover it

with the white eyeshadow, powder or make-up Even cover your lips.

Now carefully paint your eyebrows black, using the black eyeliner. Next close one eye and carefully draw a black line round it using your eyelashes as a guide. Keep your eye closed until the eyeliner is dry. Do the same with other eye.

Use the grey eyeshadow next to make larger circles round your eyes. Use the grey eyeshadow also to make your cheeks look hollow. Suck in your cheeks and fill the oval formed on each side of your face with the grey. You can make your nose look thinner too by rubbing some grey down the sides of it.

Using the black eyeliner paint a wider, thinner mouth on your face than your own mouth. This will make it look more frightening.

The final part of the make-up are the teeth. These are made from shaping the cheese wax or plasticine into two fangs. The fangs should be stuck to the two teeth that are third from the centre on your upper jaw. You must make sure that both these teeth are dry before trying to stick on the fangs. If the teeth are moist then the fangs will not stay put.

For the Dracula costume you should really have black evening dress. But since this is not very common today you can make do very well with a pair of black trousers, a white shirt, a white bow tie and a black cape.

To make the cape cut a piece of black material into a semi-circle, with the straight edge about one hundred and fifty centimetres long. In the middle of the straight edge cut a smaller semi-circle for the back of your neck. Stitch some black ribbon or shoe laces to this edge so that you can tie it round your neck and you will be all set to prowl the night as the most famous vampire of them all.

You can remove the make-up with cold cream and finish with a wash in soap and water. The wax fangs will just pull off.

Dissolving monster

The dissolving monster is a gruesome sight indeed. Its face seems to be slipping off its head and all who see it have the horrifying thought, 'What is underneath?'! Of course the answer is you, but who is to know that if your make-up is really effective?

To make-up as the dissolving monster you will need: spirit gum, or other glue which is safe for the skin; cotton-wool balls; dried peas or beans; some food colouring; flour and water; and syrup.

Start the make-up by pinning your hair back from your face. Then, using the gum, stick some of the cotton-wool balls onto your face in clumps.

Some can go above your eyes on your forehead. Others can go on your cheeks and chin. Try to make the pattern uneven, so that your face becomes bulgy and lumpy in one or two places.

Now put the dried beans or peas, and 150 grammes of flour into a bowl and add two table-spoons of syrup and water. Stir this mixture until it is a thick paste. Add the food colouring of your choice to make it a nice monster colour.

When the cotton wool balls are securely fixed to your face use a spoon or a cooking spatula to stick

the mixture from the bowl to your face. Start by putting the mixture on your forehead and then gradually move down to cover the whole of your face. Make sure that you do not get it in your eyes, though. Of course the mixture will drip, so you will have to try to stop it all sliding off your face. Tilting your head backwards should help prevent this. It might also be a good idea to put an old towel round your shoulders – just in case! Sit in a chair with your head held back until the mixture dries. You can use a hairdryer, but be careful not to get it too close to your face in case it gets too hot.

The result of all this effort should be terrifying when you have finished. You might dress yourself in some clothes that are too big for you. These will make the monster really look as if it is shrinking and dissolving, when they flap and hang loosely round your body.

When you take off the make-up, stand over a dustbin or a large sheet of newspaper and peel off as much as you can. The rest should wash off. Then if your face feels rather tight or dry, just rub in a little cold cream.

Skinless monster

The skinless monster is covered with a sickly, shiny film. This can be any colour you choose, but red or green look very good. The monster's film is lumpy and uneven which makes it look like a huge scar covering its body. Of course if you wear gloves and long-sleeved clothes, the only visible part of the monster will be its face, but when people see that they will think it looks like this all over!

To make-up as the skinless monster you will need: gelatine (unflavoured); food colouring; black eyeliner; cold cream; and water.

As with other make-ups start this one by pinning back your hair.

Now you must prepare the gelatine very carefully; in fact it would probably be best to get the cook of the household to help you, especially as you will have to use her kitchen equipment. Ask her to boil some water for you and then let it cool just a little. Put one teaspoon of the gelatine into a paper cup, add one drop of whatever food colouring you have chosen and then add one teaspoon of the hot water. Mix all this up quickly because it will cool very fast and you have to use it before it sets.

When the mixture has cooled smear it onto your face and push it around so that it is lumpy and uneven. Then mix up another teaspoon of gelatine, with some more colouring and hot water, and do the same again.

Gradually cover your whole face with the gelatine, mixing and using a little at a time. *But* be very careful about the hot water *and* be very careful not to get any of the mixture in your eyes.

In fact, it is a good idea to leave a ring round your eyes free from the gelatine mixture. When you have finished the 'monster's film', you can use the eyeliner to make two ghostly, ghastly rings round its eyes.

When you come to taking off the make-up, do not let it fall down the plug-hole: if it does, it could block up the drain, which would not please anyone. Put it in the bin or on the compost heap. The gelatine should peel off without any trouble, and soap and warm water will also remove it. The eyeliner can be removed by using cold cream and tissues. And again, if your face feels tight and dry after taking off the make-up, rub in a little cold cream.

Zombie

The most frightening thing about zombies is that they look almost like living people. They do not have strange, monster-like features, nor do they have ugly scars, or fangs like other monsters. In fact, zombies look like ordinary people because they once were ordinary people. But the real difference is that zombies are the walking dead! Their faces are drained of blood. Their eyes have a frightening stare that seems to look right through everyone else. They never speak, they never blink, and they never seem to breathe. They just move through life with deathly, pale faces and dead, glassy eyes.

To make up as a zombie you will need: white eyeshadow or powder; black eyeliner; grey eyeshadow; and cold cream.

Start by drawing your hair back from your face, holding it in place with hair pins if necessary. Rub a little cold cream into your skin. Now cover your whole face, including your lips, with the white eyeshadow or powder.

Use your finger to rub two large grey rings round your eyes, using the grey eyeshadow. Try to make the rings equal in size, and equal in shape, round each eye.

Next use the black eyeliner to paint your eyebrows jet black. You can make your eyebrows any shape you like to alter your own appearance, though here again it is better to make them match each other.

To make the zombie's eyes really stand out draw black lines round the eyes, using the eyelashes as a guide. Close each eye as you do this and make sure that you do not get any eyeliner into either eye.

The next thing to do is to make the zombie look hollow-cheeked. You can do this by finding your cheekbone and drawing a line just below it, from a point about two and a half centimetres from your nostril. Using the grey eyeshadow, draw this line with your finger towards the middle of your ear.

Then draw another line with your finger, this time from the end of your cheekbone nearest your nose, down your face to a point about two and a half centimetres away from the corner of your mouth. Draw the final line from the bottom of this second line up across your cheek to just below your ear. Now fill in the area you have marked with grey eyeshadow, and do the same with the other cheek.

Paint your mouth thinner than your own lips and use the black eyeliner to make it look frightening. If you want to, you can paint one tooth black to indicate some decay. *But* if you do this be certain that you only use *non-toxic* make-up. Your tooth will also need to be completely dry before the black make-up sticks to it.

Zombies wear any clothes you care to dress them in. If they are old and rumpled the effect will be more realistic, though, and some muddy stains will show people that you have indeed just crawled out of the grave.

To remove the make-up, use cold cream and tissues, followed by soap and water.

Ghoulish giggles

What time is it when a monster smashes down your front-door?
Time to get a new door.

When a vampire telephones an undertaker's office, what is the most important thing he asks them?
'Do you deliver?'

Where do all the biggest monsters in North America live?
In Lake Eerie.

What is the monsters' favourite building in the world?
The Vampire State Building in New York.

What is the best way to talk to a monster?
Long distance.

Why do monsters keep on forgetting what you tell them?
Because what you say goes in one ear and out of the others.

What is a monster's normal eyesight?
20–20–20–20.

What happens when you cross the Invisible Man with Frankenstein?
You get a crime wave.

What do you call a vampire's son?
A bat boy.

Where do monsters study?
At a ghoulege.

What sort of stew do monsters prefer?
Yes, you guessed right – ghoulash.

Why did King Kong climb to the top of the Empire State Building?
To catch a plane.

Fiendish fun and games

horrifying home entertainment

Here are eleven ghoulish games to play with your family and fiends.

Sound the alarm

The object of this game is to sound the alarm to warn. the villagers that the monster has escaped from the castle dungeon. However, the alarm bell is now guarded by the monster and in order to ring it you have to creep up terribly quietly. If you make the slightest noise the monster will hear you and you will join the other victims in its larder. The monster cannot see, but it has very sharp hearing.

To play the game the villagers sit round in a circle. In the middle of the circle sits the monster, blindfolded. The village watchman stands outside the circle and points to whichever villager he wants to try to sound the alarm. The alarm itself should be a small bell (but anything which makes an alarm noise will do). This is placed just in front of the monster.

When all the villagers are safely in their houses asleep (sitting quietly on the ground), the watchman will point to the first one who must try to sound the alarm. This villager then has to try to creep forward and sound the alarm without the monster hearing.

If the monster hears a noise it must point in the direction it thinks the noise came from. If it is right, the watchman says 'One more for the larder', and the villager who was creeping forward must return to his house as a ghost. Then another villager will have to try to sound the alarm.

But if the monster points in the wrong direction the villager can carry on creeping forward. Once the alarm has been sounded, the village is safe, the round is over and the villager who sounded the alarm becomes the next monster and starts another round.

Monster wounds

Everyone who has been the victim of a monster's attack and who has lived to tell the tale has quite a tale to tell. In this game they have their chance.

Each player invents his, or her, own horror story about the wound that they received and the scar they still carry to prove it. They keep the story to themselves, though. Instead of telling it, they write down the three most important words that describe what happened on a card, or piece of paper. Supposing that you had been attacked by a vampire while taking a shortcut through the graveyard late one night, you would write on the card, shortcut – graveyard – vampire. On the other hand you might have been gashed by the claws of one of the monsters guarding the Mummy's tomb, in which case you might write Mummy's tomb – fight – monster guard.

When all the players have filled in their cards they are placed face down on a table in a pile.

The players then divide into pairs and they draw scars and other wounds on each other's hands, arms, faces, or legs. (To draw the wounds you can use an eyebrow pencil, but *do* make sure that you put a little cold cream on the site of the wound first. If you don't it will be there longer than you want!)

When every player is scarred and wounded, the game can begin. One player is chosen to start and he, or she, pulls any card from the pile, and, then, looking in a mirror at his, or her, own scar, tells the others how he, or she, was wounded, using the three key words on the card to build up the story.

The person on the player's right goes next and so the game continues until every player has told his or her own gory horror story.

146

Swamp stretching

In this game the players are stranded in the middle of a deadly swamp. The only means of escape is to stretch as far as possible across the swamp and place a land-anchor on firm ground. However, the monster that lives in the swamp can move as soon as it hears one prisoner escaping, which means that all the others are eaten alive as soon as the first prisoner has got away! The other difficulty is that no one knows how far away firm land is, so only the prisoner who can reach the furthest can try to escape, because if the land-anchor is stuck in soft ground, it might give way when anyone tries to pull him or herself through the swamp on a rope attached to it.

To play the game all the players (prisoners) stand against one wall. A footstool, or a strong box, is placed against the wall and it is from this that all the escape attempts have to be made.

Each player is then given a land-anchor (an empty matchbox). Now, taking it in turns, they have to try to place this as far away from the wall as they can. However, they have to keep both feet on the stool or box all the time, and they are only allowed to touch the floor with their hands, because these are protected from the swamp by special gloves. If their knees, chests, elbows or heads touch the floor, then they will sink in the swamp and die.

When they have reached out as far as they can, they leave their land-anchor on that spot. They cannot throw it, because it would not stick in the ground firmly enough, so they have to leave it only as far as their hand will reach.

After every player has made a bid for escape, see which one has stretched furthest to safety. The one who has, becomes the lucky prisoner who can try to pull himself, or herself, through the swamp to safety.

Of course if there is one very tall prisoner to begin with he has to drop out right away because the swamp monster always eats the tallest first. After all, the tallest are the most likely to escape. But it's not always so. Strong arms are more important in this game than long arms. You try it and see.

(The player who drops out is the judge of the other bids for escape.)

Hide the charm

The charm in this game is a ring. But it is no ordinary ring. It is the ring which protects all the players from vampires. However, the charm only protects them when the vampire does not know which player has it. As soon as it finds out who has the charm, all the other players are at risk, because they are no longer protected, and the vampire can attack them without fear for itself.

The game is played with the vampire in the centre of a circle of string. This has to be a long piece of string as it must reach round the circle formed by all the other players. On the string is the magic charm (the ring – a curtain-ring will do). And the object of the game is for the players to pass the ring from one fist to another without the vampire seeing them do it. The players slide their hands backwards and forwards on the string, sometimes collecting the ring and some-times not. They keep their hands moving all the time, even if they are not actually passing the ring. This helps to confuse the vampire.

The vampire has to watch the hands carefully. When it guesses correctly where the ring is, and which player has it, then the vampire has won, and the player who had the ring becomes the vampire in the centre for the next round.

Siamese monster game

You probably know that Siamese twins are born with their bodies joined together. But you may not know that, deep in the jungles of Siam, there used to live a Siamese monster that also had two bodies. The monster's bodies were joined at what we would call the forehead. This meant that the monster could only move sideways, and in this game the players pretend to be Siamese monsters and move as quickly as they can.

To play this game there have to be an even number of players because two players are needed to make each monster; and the minimum number of players is four, so that two monsters can race against each other.

Once the players have been divided into pairs each pair is given a tennis ball or an orange. You may wonder what this has got to do with the monster. Well, the answer is that the monster is formed by the two players holding the ball or the orange between their foreheads, which means they have to press their heads together with the ball or orange in between.

When the monsters are ready they have to line up on one side of a room. Then when the word 'Go' is given, they have to race to the other side of the room and back again as quickly as they can. But they must keep the ball in place all the time they are racing. If it slips and falls to the floor it means that the monster has lost its only eye and cannot see where it is going. When this happens it has to go back to the beginning, and start all over again with the ball once more in place.

The first monster to complete the course without losing its eye is the winner. It may sound quite easy, but just you try to do it!

Grim-faced monster game

Have you noticed that very few monsters smile?
Most of them have frightening faces which always
look grim and terrifying. Well in this game the
idea is to remain a grim-faced monster even
though you might want to burst out laughing.

The monsters do not pull funny faces or try to
appear ugly. That is not the object of the game.
What they have to do is to keep a completely
blank expression all the time.

This is not as easy as it sounds, because each
monster has to try to make the others smile or
laugh.

To begin with the monsters all sit round in a
close circle. Then one that has been chosen to
start turns to the monster on its right and does
something to it. It may touch the monster's nose,
tickle it behind the ear, pinch its toes, or do
anything it likes to make the monster laugh. Then
this monster turns to the one on its right and does
the same thing, and so the action is passed round
the circle from one monster to the other until it
comes back to the one who started. That monster
then does something else to the monster on its
right, and so the game continues.

Any monster which smiles or loses its grim face,
even for a moment, either leaves the game, or
pays a forfeit of some sort.

Hold off the Body Snatchers

The Body Snatchers have invaded the earth and the only way of stopping them from carrying out their evil errand is to form a circle round the body and try to keep them out.

In this game one player is chosen to be the Body Snatcher and another is chosen to be the body. The other players then join arms to form a protective circle round the body, while the Body Snatcher stands on the outside of this ring.

The idea of the game is for the Body Snatcher to break through the circle and snatch the body. But the players in the circle have to try to keep the Body Snatcher away. It has to try to break through the circle, crawl under the locked arms, trick the players in the circle and then dart in when they are not expecting it, in fact it can use any way of trying to snatch the body.

When the Body Snatcher finally succeeds, the two players who broke the circle then become the body and the Body Snatcher, and another round begins.

Ghostly moans

In spite of its name this game can be great fun at a party. Often people only hear ghosts moaning in

152

the dark, without being able to see them. In this game the victim has to try to identify the ghosts by the sound of their moans.

One player is chosen as a victim. He, or she, is then blindfolded to recreate the darkness. Then once the blindfold is in place, all the other players sit round in a circle, with the victim in the middle.

The victim walks round the circle and sits on the lap of one of the ghosts, but does not touch this ghost in any other way at all.

The victim then makes a moaning noise and the ghost has to reply by making three moaning noises and ghostly cries in reply. When the victim has heard the ghost's moans and cries he must try to identify him. If he names the wrong ghost or can't guess at all, he drops out of the game altogether and the ghost whose identity wasn't guessed becomes the new victim, putting on the blindfold, walking round the circle and sitting on somebody's lap. If the victim guesses the ghost's name correctly, then it is the ghost who drops out of the game and leaves the circle while the victim moves on to another ghost's lap and starts moaning and guessing all over again. The last two players left playing the game are the winners.

Prisoners in the tomb

The tomb is a large, underground vault. Two daring explorers have ventured inside, further than any men have dared to go before. But the guardian of the tomb has trapped them inside and only one has any chance of escape. The other will be kept and fed to the monster who lives deep in the maze of tunnels which lead from the tomb.

The tomb is pitch black. There is no light inside and the explorers have to rely on their senses of sound and touch. However, the guardian of the tomb gives them a sporting chance to get away. It tosses the keys of the door to the tomb onto the floor so that the two explorers have to feel for them. The first to find the keys is the one to escape. The other becomes the monster's next meal!

To play the game you have to recreate the total darkness of the tomb, but in order to enjoy the fun, the best way of doing this is not to draw the curtains, but to blindfold the two prisoners.

When they are blindfolded, stand them facing each other, three or four paces apart. Now the player who has been chosen as the guardian of the tomb makes an eerie moaning sound and then throws the large jangling key ring with its bunch of noisy keys somewhere on the floor between them. Just before it throws the keys the guardian must say in a ghastly voice, 'Mortal men your time has come, find the keys or die.' Then it must toss them onto the floor.

As soon as the explorers hear the key ring clatter on the floor they have to try to find it and pick it up.

The first one to succeed is allowed to escape. The other goes to be the monster. The escaper wins one point.

Then two more explorers are chosen and blindfolded and another round is played.

After a set number of rounds the explorer with the highest score wins.

Zombies

As you know, zombies are those frightening creatures which were once newly buried bodies. However, they have been dug out of their graves by a sorcerer before they became skeletons and now walk the earth like people in a sleep-walk. The sorcerer has complete power over them and the zombies silently obey every action or command he gives.

In this game one player is chosen as the sorcerer, another player is the detective, and all the others are the zombies.

The detective is sent out of the room to begin with, because his purpose is to discover which of the other players is the sorcerer. When he is out of the room, the sorcerer is chosen, and he and the zombies spread themselves about the room. The detective is then called back into the room.

To play the game the sorcerer makes all sorts of different motions. He might raise one leg, pat his head, touch his knee, or clench his fist, but whatever he does the zombies have to do the same thing. The sorcerer must only perform one motion at a time. But when he changes from one to another the zombies must change with him.

However, they must avoid looking directly at the sorcerer, because if they do, the detective will know right away who he is. The secret of the game is for all the players to move so closely in time that it is very difficult for the detective to discover which of them is giving the lead to the others.

Once the detective discovers the identity of the sorcerer, the sorcerer becomes the detective and leaves the room, while the others choose a new sorcerer and the game starts again.

Steal the monster's treasure

In this game the monster is invisible, but its treasure is not. Its treasure is so precious that everyone wants to steal it. However, in their greed the people divide into two groups and they compete against each other to steal the treasure.

To play the game you will need a large space; a

school gym, or a playground would be ideal, but it's also a good game for the garden.

A leader is chosen from among the players and the others then divide into two equal-sized teams. If there are an even number of players, then choose two leaders to even the numbers in the teams.

When the teams have been chosen each person in each team is given a number, which he or she has to remember, so that there will be one person in each team who is number 1, for example, and one person in each team who is number 2, 3, 4 and so on.

The teams then line up on their boundary lines, which should be about ten metres apart. The treasure (a ball, a shoe, a cardboard box) is then placed between them.

Now the leader calls out one of the numbers. The two players whose number has been called then dash towards the treasure and try to bring it back across their boundary line. When one player snatches the treasure, the other has to try to tag him or her before they reach the safety of their boundary.

If the player who has stolen the treasure reaches his or her boundary without having been tagged, then that team gets two points. If the player is tagged though, the other team gets one point.

The treasure is then put back in the middle and another round is played. The team with the most points at the end wins.

Ghoulish giggles

Who looks after monsters in a football team?
The ghoulkeeper.

Where do monsters go for their holidays?
To the ghoast.

What's the best way of describing monster films?
Spooktacular!

What part of a dance do vampires like best?
The last vaults.

Which bears do ghouls like best?
Pall-bears.

What happened to Frankenstein when he lost his hand?
He went io a second-hand shop.

What do monsters do every evening at dusk?
They take a coffin break.

What's King Kong's favourite snack?
A godzilla cheese sandwich.

Which monster eats faster than any other?
The goblin.

Why did Frankenstein marry his bride?
Because he had a crush on her.

Why is Dracula a good guest to take out to dinner?
Because he eats necks to nothing.

What should you do when you find a green monster in your garden?
Wait until he ripens.

Make a monster

How to build yourself a monster

Monster masks, monster models, monster puppets, monster costumes – everything you need to make yourself a monster quite as terrifying as anything created by Dr Frankenstein.

Simple monster mask

This is a basic mask which you can use to make any monster mask you wish. Once you have made the mask you can decorate it in any way you like, using any materials you like, to create new and strange monsters which the world has never seen before.

To make this mask you will need: a balloon; tissue paper; vaseline; newspaper; wallpaper paste; elastic; and string or wool.

To begin with, blow up the balloon and stand it in a container which will hold it firm while you work on it – a jam jar will do.

Smear vaseline all over the surface of the balloon and then cover the entire surface with small pieces of tissue paper.

Now tear the newspaper into long thin strips and stick these onto the balloon with the wall-paper paste. Make sure that you overlap these strips and make sure too that you do not leave any creases on the surface.

You will need to put on four or more layers of these strips. So be certain to use lots of paste and put all the layers on in quick succession.

Now you will have to wait for a week while the layers dry thoroughly. If you put the balloon in a warm place, near the boiler or near a radiator (but not too near!), this will speed up the drying process.

Once all the layers have dried right through, burst the balloon and pull it out of the hole in the bottom of the mask.

You should now be left with a paper 'egg-shell'. You can do two things with this. You can either cut it in half, down the middle, to give yourself two masks, or else you can cut away just enough to let you slip it over your head.

What you will have to do in either case is to cut two holes for your eyes, a hole for your nose and some sort of hole for your mouth.

From then on the decoration is up to you. You can stick on pieces of wool or string as hair. You can stick on plastic cups, or cardboard paper-rolls to make a nose, tusks or horns. And of course you can paint the mask in any number of ways.

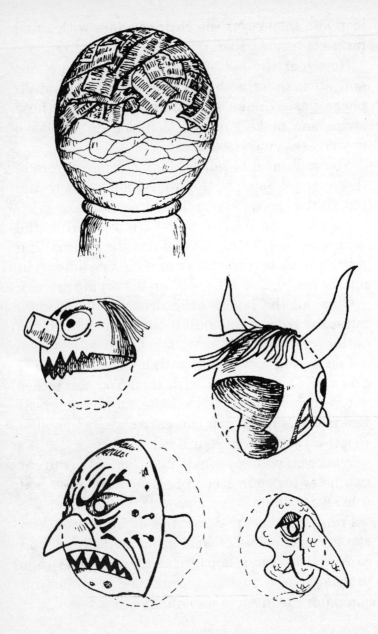

Pieces of elastic round your ears or round the back of your head will help keep the mask in place and prevent it from slipping just at the moment when you are about to give some unsuspecting victim the fright of his life.

Devil heads

Devil heads are another test of your imagination and your artistic skill. Once you have mastered the essential technique of making them you can create monsters all of your own. You could even start a monster zoo if you wanted to.

This is what you will need to make the monstrous heads: cardboard cartons; cardboard egg boxes; wallpaper paste; ordinary cardboard; glue; sellotape and paint.

The first operation is to make a nice messy cardboard pulp. To do this, break up the egg boxes into lots of little pieces and put them into a bucket of water to soak. You will need to leave them there all night to make sure that they are properly soaked. But the following day you should be able to tip out the water that's left and then mix the paper into a pulp, being careful to remove any lumps.

To complete the pulp mixture you must add the wallpaper paste. Mix in about one part of paste to three parts of pulp. This should turn the mixture into a substance that you can easily mould with your hands.

Each devil head is built up on a base, so before starting with your work of art, you will have to make the base for it. For this you can use the cardboard cartons. Take two of these and make a sort of newspaper sandwich with them. That is to say screw up sheets of newspaper, lay them between the two layers of cardboard and then press the whole sandwich firmly together. Stick sellotape over the sides to hold it tightly together.

Once you have done this you can start to make your monster. Put a lump of the doughy pulp onto the base you have made and start to shape the monster's head. Gradually build up the beast's profile, adding tusks, eyes, noses, warts and horns as you progress. If you want to, you can cut the ordinary cardboard into the shape of huge horns, like a unicorn's horn for example. These can be stuck to the face with glue, once the face itself has dried.

You will have to be patient while the pulp is drying out thoroughly, but it will be worth waiting for. It is probably a good idea to make several monsters at once, so that when they are all dry you will have several models to decorate.

Use the paint to colour the monster, but if you use spray paints be careful where you point them; cover the floor or table with old newspaper and make certain that you do not get any paint in your eyes. Even better, spray the paint carefully out-of-doors.

Janus masks

Janus was the Roman god of doorways. He had two faces, one looking forwards the other looking backwards. In ancient Rome, Janus was believed to stand at the doorway of the year, looking backwards at the year which was coming to an end and looking forwards to the year which was about to begin. As a consequence we still call the first month of the year January after this Roman god.

You can make a Janus mask in two easy ways Traditionally one face was smiling while the other was sad, but you can give your faces any expression you like.

The simplest Janus mask actually has four faces because you make it out of a cardboard box.

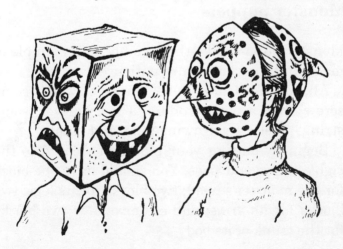

All you have to do is paint four faces, one on each side of the box, and then cut eye-holes in one of the faces so that you can see where you are going.

In the second method you will have to make a simple monster mask, as described earlier. Once you have cut the mask in half, decide how you are going to decorate it. Perhaps you want to leave the mask as it is and just paint a face on each side? On the other hand you might want to stick on a nose, ears, a pointed chin, horns and lots of hair?

Whichever way you decorate it, you will have to cut eye slits in the mask at the front so that you can see where you are going. You will also have to attach the two sides of the mask together. A piece of elastic, or a rubber band, on each side of your head is as good a way as any.

Monster puppets

Monster puppets like these can be fairly simple to make, but they do require patience.

All you need are: some blocks of wood; some screw eyes; a pair of pliers; a screwdriver; some string; plasticine; drawing pins; and paint.

Begin by cutting your blocks of wood into the right shapes and sizes. You should have one block for the monster's head; two blocks for its legs; two blocks for its arms; and either one or two blocks for the trunk of its body.

166

When you have cut the blocks, sand them smooth with sand paper and lay them in their right position on a flat surface.

You must use the screw eyes to attach the limbs and head to the monster's body. So screw one screw eye into the head and each of the limbs. Then carefully open each of the eyes with a screwdriver so that there is just enough space to slip them over another screw eye.

Now screw more screw eyes into the trunk of the monster's body. (If it has two parts to its trunk you will need a screw eye in each section in order to join the two parts together.) When all the screw eyes are in position, carefully attach the head and the limbs to the trunk, closing the open screw eyes with a pair of pliers each time.

Now, using drawing pins or sellotape, attach the control strings to the monster's limbs and its head, with one string to control each part. The other ends of these strings should then be attached to a cross frame, as in the drawing. However, the two strings attached to the monster's feet must be secured to a separate piece of wood. This can then either be carried on the cross frame, held in place by a peg (or screw), or else it can be taken off and operated independently by the other hand to make the monster walk.

The decoration of the monster is a matter of your choice. The plasticine is useful for moulding the square wooden blocks into more unusual monster

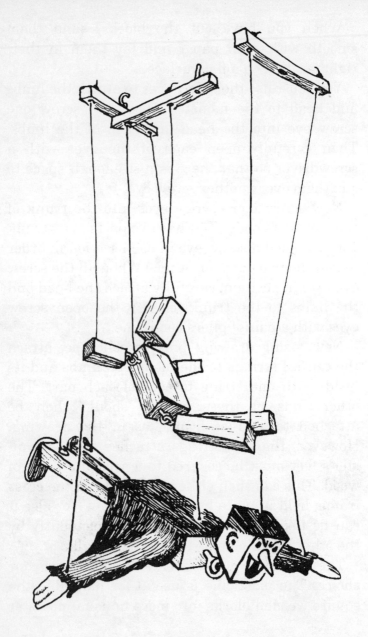

shapes. And you can use paint to colour the monster to your own taste. If you decide to make clothes for the monster be sure that they do not interfere with the way in which you operate it.

Start by making a small monster. Then when you are familiar with the puppet's construction you can make monsters as big as you like, provided that you can pick them up of course!

Monster from the deep

Sea monsters and the creatures that live in the ocean depths are among the most frightening that we are ever likely to meet. Remember *Jaws*? And that was a fish that we all knew. So imagine the fright that people will get when they are confronted by a new and totally unexpected monster from the deep.

To make this particular monster you will need: white cardboard; plasticine; vaseline; wallpaper paste; old newspapers; some pieces of uncooked macaroni; dried beans or peas; sellotape; and green wrapping paper, or crêpe paper.

The first thing to do is to prepare the mould for the monster's face. If you do this carefully you ought to be able to use the mould more than once. So it is worth spending some time making it properly. Take the sheet of cardboard and cut it into an oval shape that is wider and higher than your own face. Hold the oval to your face and mark your nose, your eyes and your mouth. Also mark the bottom of your chin and the top of your forehead.

Now cut V-shaped slits from the edge of the cardboard to these two last marks and then cut out holes for your nose, your eyes and your mouth.

The next thing to do is to bend the cardboard into the shape of the monster's face. To do this, stick together the edges of the two V-shapes at the top and bottom of the cardboard mask, with sellotape. This will make the mask curve. Place the curved cardboard over an upturned oval cereal bowl covered with tin foil or some similar material. Tape the cardboard to the bowl and then place both on a good-sized sheet of newspaper.

The next thing to do is shape the ridges in the monster's face. You use the plasticine for this. Start by rolling long sausages of plasticine slightly thicker than your two thumbs placed together.

Lay the first sausage along the ridge of the monster's nose, from a point between its eyes, to a point just above the mouth hole. Then lay one long piece from one side of the mask to the other, running just above the mouth and joining the piece that forms the nose. Lastly take two sausages and attach these like huge curved eyebrows, one above each eye. They should join the top of the nose piece and then curve away to the side of the mask, near where the top of your ear would be. Now your mould is completed.

Once you have done this you can start to build the monster's hideous mask. But before you begin you *must* smear vaseline over the whole of the mask, covering both the plasticine and the cardboard. This is terribly important: if you do not do this then the mask will become stuck to the mould and you will never be able to get it off!

The actual mask is made in the same way as the simple monster mask, using strips of newspaper and wallpaper paste. Tear the newspaper into long thin strips about two centimetres wide and twenty centimetres long. Use the paste to glue them in place on the mould, laying the strips from side to side, and making sure that each strip overlaps the previous one. Start at the bottom of the mask and work your way up systematically to the monster's forehead. Be sure that you press the paper well into the contours of the monster's face. But at the same time do not press too hard or you might damage the mould.

When you have covered the whole face with several layers of strips running from side to side, finish off with three strips, one running along the nose and one running along each of the eyebrows.

Finally, before you leave the mask to dry, take your pieces of macaroni and stick them into the ridge that ran above the monster's mouth. This is to make holes for the real teeth when the mask has dried.

The mask will take a few days to dry. You must

be patient and wait until it has dried right through. If you try to move it too soon, it may fall to pieces and you will only succeed in spoiling the result of all your hard work.

Removing the mask from the mould is a very tricky business. Begin by lifting the mask and mould, still attached to each other, from the sheet of paper underneath. Next cut the sellotape holding the bowl and foil to the cardboard and plasticine above it. Now you are ready to ease the mask away from the cardboard and plasticine mould, using a blunt knife. Once the mask is free, clean up the inside and trim the edges to make it smooth.

As a finishing touch to the mask construction bind the edges all the way round with one or two strips of paper and paste. This will give an even, tidy finish.

Now you can start to decorate the monster. Begin by sticking the dried beans or peas all over the monster's face like horrible warts. Paint the whole face a ghastly sea-green when the glue has dried.

When the paint is dry glue macaroni teeth into the holes that you made earlier. Make the ends of the macaroni that stick out of the monster's mask jagged and rough; this will make it look even more frightening. Lastly attach a piece of elastic, or two rubber bands, to the mask to fix it on to your head.

You can use the green paper to make seaweed. Cut it into long thin strips and glue them to the top of the mask so that they hang down across the monster's face and head.

Now you will have a devilish-looking mask which no one will be able to see without it sending a shudder down their spine. Happy prowling!

King Kong

This is a simple way of making yourself a King Kong costume. Although we only show you how to make the mask and hands hairy, you can if you want make the whole body hairy, but this will take much longer and be much more expensive. Why not try following these instructions first? You can always be more ambitious a second time.

To make the monster's costume you will need: a balloon; vaseline; newspapers; wallpaper paste; a lot of old rope and string, the hairier the better; an old sack; and some black poster paint.

Start by making a simple monster head as previously directed, using the balloon, the wall-paper paste and the newspaper strips.

When the mask has fully dried, pop the balloon and remove it, then cut the mask into two equal parts. Cut the bottom off one of the two halves and stick this a little below the middle of the other half to make the monster's chin. Pack this with screwed-up newspaper to hold the chin in place. Attach a piece of elastic, or two rubber bands, to the sides of the mask and try it on your head for size.

Using a pencil, mark where the eye holes and nose hole should be while it is on your head, then remove it and carefully cut these out with the point of a pair of scissors.

Once you have completed this basic mask you can start to make the monster's hair, using the rope and string. The best sort of rope to use is hemp, because this is naturally hairy. Likewise a hairy type of string is better than the smoother sorts that are available. You will need to cut the rope and string into lengths between twelve and six centimetres long. If you can find a steel comb, like the sort used for grooming dogs, this will help you fluff up the string and rope into the monster's hair and fur.

When you have prepared your hair, stick it to the monster's mask as untidily as you like, so that it has a rough shaggy appearance. Make sure that you cover all the mask, though; do not leave any bald patches. Also try to have some hair that falls back from the top of the mask which will blend in with your own hair when you are wearing the costume.

To make the monster's hands hairy you can use a pair of old rubber gloves. Again stick the hair at random to these, allowing some of it to hang loosely from each hand, especially from the back of the hand. Look at pictures of monkeys and apes to get an idea of how the hair is distributed on their hands.

By the time you have made King Kong's hands, your mask should have dried. So now you can add the finishing touches by outlining its eyes with the black paint and painting in its mouth.

The rest of the costume is very straightforward. Just cut slits in the sides of the sack for your head and arms and put it over your head. Slip the mask over your head, put on the gloves and away you go to prowl the neighbourhood and perhaps even climb the Empire State Building, who knows?

One-eyed monster

You can turn yourself into this gruesome specimen by using only a few simple materials. In fact, all you will need is: a ping-pong ball; some pink plasticine; a bandage; and different coloured felt-tipped pens.

You use the ping-pong ball to make the monster's eye. Begin by carefully cutting it in half and smoothing off any rough edges. Now draw the pupil of the monster's eye with pens and make it look as horrible as you can.

Next, roll the plasticine into two strips about as wide as your thumbs put together and as long as the two of them joined end to end. These strips will be used to attach the eye to your forehead. Use one above the eye and one below it to hold the half ping-pong ball in place. If the plasticine does not stick securely to your forehead, use a little spirit gum or other *safe* glue to hold it in place.

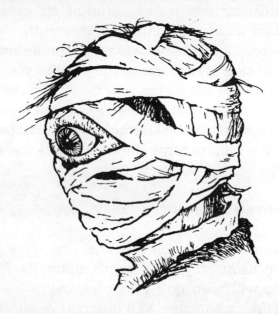

Once the monster's eye is securely fixed to your forehead you can start to cover your face with the bandage. Wind it round your head making sure that the monster's eye is not covered, and making sure too that you leave tiny chinks in the bandage so that you can see out yourself.

When you have secured the bandage use the rest of the plasticine to make warts in the monster's skin. As a finishing touch pull a few strands of hair out from underneath the bandage to make the monster look really untidy.

Ghoulish giggles

What's the name of the overweight monster that lives at the Opera House?
The Fat-tum of the Opera.

What do monsters like so much about horse riding?
Ghoulloping.

Which day of the week do monsters like best?
Moanday.

Why was Frankenstein the monster so fond of Dr Frankenstein, his inventor?
Because he kept him in stitches.

What did the vampires call false teeth when they first saw a set?
A new-fangled device.

What did the headless horseman do when he lost his head?
He rode off to look for the head hunter.

What's the game that vampires like best?
Bat-minton.

What do you call a witch that goes on holiday to the sea, but never goes in the water?
A chicken sand witch.

What do you call a clean, good-looking, friendly, kindly monster?
A failure.

How do you raise a baby monster when you find one left by its parents?
With a hydraulic jack.

Which monster has feathers, fangs, wings and webbed feet?
Count Duckula.

How do skeletons eat mashed potato?
In gravy.

Frankenstein's scrapbook

There are so many different types of monster and so many different things they do that it is difficult to keep track of them half the time. That is why it is such a good idea to keep a scrapbook of all the bits of information or ideas which you pick up about monsters.

The nice thing about a scrapbook is that you can enter things in any order. If you find a picture of Frankenstein in a magazine, you can cut this out and paste it into your scrapbook next to a magic spell that you have to chant if you want to become a werewolf, and no one will mind at all. In fact it will make your scrapbook more interesting if you include random entries.

So, here are a few suggestions of topics which you might include in your scrapbook. But these are just to get you going. You ought to be able to find lots of different pieces of information about monsters, and you will find that one idea will lead you on to another, and that in turn will lead you to another one, and so on.

Your own inspiration

I have to admit that these are not my own inspiration, they are better than that. These are the work of some of the pupils at Orwell Park School which I visited not long ago.

The poems are their own, but the inspiration for them came from reading about monsters or seeing monsters on television. We all get inspired by things we see and read, and sometimes we are so moved that we want to capture our feelings in a poem or a story. If you have ever been really frightened by a monster film or television programme, or better still by a monster story which you have read or been told, then you ought to try to express what you felt on paper.

You can either describe your own feelings, or you can make up a story of your own, using scenes or monsters from the original story to make your own one really scary and spooky.

Look at these examples and see how it can be done:

Horror

At the end-of the day,
I hear a ghostly horse neigh,
In the night I hear rattling skeletons,
Knocking on my wellingtons,

The floorboards creak,
And someone screams above me,
Suddenly a glaring light beams upon me,
I hear bangs;
I see fangs;
I try to start fighting,
But he starts biting,
There is a flood of blood,
A headless horse-man gallops past,
But then it is morning at last.
Phew! It was only a dream.

Alexander Ravenshear

Haunted castle

In I creep.
The door slams shut with a bang.
At every step I take there is a loud creak.
'Screech, Screech' – bats swoop past.
I walk up to a door. It opens by itself.
From down below comes a blood-curdling scream.
I creep down the stairs.
Suddenly there is a wave of evil laughter.
I get to the bottom and see GHOSTS!
Ghosts of people being tortured – people without
     heads.
I run up the stairs and hear more screams.
It dies away and then there is silence.

Michael Butler

Monsters of the screen

Probably the most common way of getting to know monsters today is by watching horror films and seeing monsters on television.

Of course, behind even the best monsters there are actors. But what makes the monsters so frighteningly real is the skill of the make-up artists and the special effects department who make all the film sets, and who take all the trick photography.

One of the interesting things about horror films is that most of the ones which are thought to be the best today are among some of the oldest; and some of these date back to the very early days of the cinema.

It is fun to collect the names of all the horror films that you can find. Even if you do not manage to see all of them, you can always try to find out who was in them, what the story of each film was, and what special effects there were in the film.

You may be able to find still photographs taken from the films in magazines about the cinema, and these would look marvellous in your scrapbook.

Here are ten of the most famous horror films ever made. Try to see how much you can find out about them (the 'Frankenstein and Friends' chapter earlier in the book will start you off on the right track):

The Cabinet of Dr Caligari	1919
The Golem	1920
Dr Jekyll and Mr Hyde	1921
Nosferatu	1921
Dracula	1931
Frankenstein	1931
The Mummy	1932
King Kong	1932–33
Werewolf of London	1935
The Body Snatcher	1945

Devote a whole double page to each film. Write down the names of the director and the leading actors, as well as your views on the film, if and when you see it. Then add as many other interesting facts or pieces of information about it that you can find.

Another interesting aspect of horror films is the actors who have become famous through playing the parts of monsters. Here again it is fun to find out as much as you can about the stars of horror films, especially as in the early years many of the greatest film monsters were played by a small group of very talented actors.

Lon Chaney

Lon Chaney was one of the best known horror actors. He was a genius with make-up and he could make his face change into so many different disguises that he became known as 'The Man of a Thousand Faces'.

He was the son of deaf parents, which might seem a disadvantage, but which turned out to be part of the secret of Lon Chaney's great film success. In the silent films of his era, the actors had to express their meaning in gestures and expressions. Since Lon Chaney had been used to doing this all his life whenever he wanted to communicate with his parents, he was very skilled by the time he came to display his talents on the screen.

He made his first film in 1920, yet ten years later he was dead. Even so he established a reputation in those years which has made him one of the great legends of the cinema.

Half-way through his film career he starred in *The Phantom of the Opera*, which is perhaps his best-known film. His make-up in this film was so effective that it really looked as if his face was a ghastly skull. In fact, Chaney is said to have filled his mouth with springs and clamps which held back his nostrils and pushed his cheeks higher than his cheekbones. Try to find a photograph of him as the phantom and you can see how effective his make-up was for yourself.

Boris Karloff

Boris Karloff was the greatest of the film Frankensteins. He had been acting in Hollywood for thirteen years before he made the film that confirmed him as the successor to Lon Chaney as the genius of make-up.

The famous Frankenstein make-up was created by Karloff and the film company's make-up man, Jack Pierce. For three weeks they worked on designs for the monster's body which has become so well known for its square skull, the electrodes in its neck, its huge hands and enormous feet. The result was a triumph, which was just as well for Karloff, who had to spend three and a half hours every morning putting on the make-up and costume. The monster's legs were made to look stiff by metal splints, and two pairs of trousers that went on top. There were clamps inside his mouth which pulled down the corners to give the monster its characteristic expression, and the huge boots which Karloff had to wear weighed over eight kilograms each.

Many people who saw the film when it first came out said that one of the reasons for its great success was that Boris Karloff gave the monster a sense of humanity. Yes, Frankenstein was frightening, but it was also tragic, and for an actor with no lines to help him this was a remarkable achievement.

Christopher Lee

After the Second World War the interest in horror films seemed to have died away until in the mid 1950s an English film company, called Hammer Films, started to re-make the horror classics in ghastly, gory, gruesome Technicolor, and a new generation of horror films was born.

With this new generation of films came a new generation of horror monster actors, the most well known being Christopher Lee.

He had been an actor for ten years, but he really found success for the first time with Hammer, for whom he played most of the leading monsters at one time or another.

His first part was Frankenstein, but he was best known for his performance as Dracula, which he played in several films for Hammer. Unlike previous Draculas, however, Christopher Lee actually showed his deadly fangs on the screen, and when he attacked his victims the blood flowed as it had never flowed on the screen before!

Bela Lugosi

Before Christopher Lee ever played Count Dracula there was only one actor the cinema public associated with the vampire. His name was Bela Lugosi.

Bela Lugosi was the first famous screen Count Dracula, which was very fitting as he had actually been born in Hungary, where vampire beliefs were very strong.

He first played Dracula on the stage, but the success of the play led to his first Dracula film which was a tremendous success. He wore very little make-up as Dracula because his own face looked so sinister. But by all accounts his Dracula must have been very convincing. Apparently there was a nurse in the audience every night to help anyone who was too frightened by the performance.

After the tremendous success of *Dracula*, Bela Lugosi was actually offered the part of Frankenstein. However, he felt that this non-speaking part was rather a come-down and he rejected it. If he had played Frankenstein, he might have combined his own success as Dracula with Boris Karloff's success as the monster. However, this was not to be.

He made more than one hundred films during his acting career, but Dracula was always considered to be his greatest role, and when he died in 1956 he was buried wrapped in the black cloak with the red satin lining which he had worn so many times as the wicked vampire.

Monster recipe

Monsters have to eat like everything else. Some of them survive on blood. Some of them enjoy tucking into a tasty lump of human flesh, and the Reptile seemed to find rats and mice very much to her liking. But most of these foods are not the sort of thing which we would enjoy eating. So here is a recipe for something which looks perfect for every monster, but which we can eat and enjoy as well – green jelly.

Green jelly is easy to make and is an enjoyable light pudding after any meal, such as rats, mice, toads, helpless maidens, or plain old fish and chips.

All you need for the jelly is about half a litre of water; half a litre packet of lemon jelly; and a little green food colouring. This will make jelly for four monsters. (Ask a grown-up for permission before you start.)

This is how you make the jelly:

Gently heat the water in a saucepan.

Put the jelly into the water and dissolve it, following the instructions on the packet. Add a few drops of green food colouring.

Let the jelly cool slightly in the saucepan.

Rinse the mould or basin in cold water. This makes it easier to turn out the jelly when it is set.

You may be able to find moulds which look like monsters. Or better still, why not try to find several moulds that look like different animals and then join them together on the plate, when their jellies have set, to make a completely original green jelly monster. It sounds revolting, but imagine the effect that it would have on your guests if you presented them with something that looked like a cross between King Kong, the monster from the deep, and a jellyfish.

Pour the jelly from the saucepan into the mould, or moulds, and leave to set in a cool place.

Once it has set take the jelly mould, or moulds, from their cool place to the kitchen table. Now rinse the serving plate under cold water and shake it to remove most of the water, but leave a damp surface. This helps the jelly to move on the plate, without breaking or sticking.

To make the jelly slightly looser in its mould, plunge it into warm water for a few seconds – no longer, or it will melt.

Now put the plate over the top of the mould so that it is firmly pressed against the base. Turn it over so that the jelly is sitting on the plate. Gently shake the mould and then lift it clear of the jelly.

To decorate the jelly and make it look really suitable for a monster's feast, you could use pieces of fruit. Cherries would make good eyes, or warts! You could use grapes in a similar way. Green apple peel cut into long thin strips makes very good decoration, *but* remember that you must *wash* the apples well before peeling them.

Try to think up your own ways of making the monster jelly as interesting and tempting – or revolting – as you can!

Perhaps there are other recipes that you can think of which monsters would enjoy? Write these down in your scrapbook. They might be very useful the next time a vampire drops in to see you. You never know, they might literally save your neck!

Secret, magic monster chants and curses

Many monsters were originally human beings. Vampires, werewolves and zombies all started life, or death, as people just like you and me. But they were transformed into their deathly shapes by the secret power of evil forces at work in the world of darkness.

Some of these monsters became monsters as a result of other people's actions. But others willingly made themselves monsters, usually with terrible results.

Many books have been written about vampires and werewolves, for example, and these would be good monsters to choose in starting to collect your own material on the evil powers at work. Some of the chants and magic rites seem like those we read about in old fairy tales. But others are far more sinister and seem very close to black magic.

Try to find out where the magic spells and secret formulae came from. Try to find out how old they are. *But*, whatever you do, be warned against trying them out on yourself. Everyone may tell you that they are just a lot of hocus-pocus but would you really want to be turned into some dreadful creature of the night, just to prove that they were wrong? I very much doubt it.

To give you an idea of the sort of things which you might find, here is a little information about the way that people in Russia used to try to make themselves werewolves.

Russia is an ideal country for anyone who fancies his or her chances as a werewolf. The country is covered with huge dark forests in which many real wolves live. So it was natural that many traditions about wolfmen should have grown up in Russia.

Midnight was the best time to try to become a werewolf and the light of the full moon was also considered to be essential.

The person wishing to become a werewolf had to prepare a special ointment at this time. The ingredients varied from one recipe to the next but essentially they included substances like opium, foxgloves, wolfsbane, fat of a newly-killed cat, bat blood and wolf hair. All these were put into a large pot and boiled while the would-be werewolf chanted.

When the mixture was properly 'cooked', the would-be werewolf rubbed the ointment all over his body. He put a piece of wolf's fur round his waist and then, looking up at the full moon, he began to chant this magic spell:

Make me a werewolf strong and bold,
The terror alike of young and old.
Grant me a figure tall and spare;
The speed of the elk, the claws of a bear;
The poison of snakes, the wit of the fox;

The jaws of the tiger, the teeth of the shark;
The eyes of a cat that sees in the dark.
Make me a werewolf! Make me a man-eater!
Make me a werewolf! Make me a man-eater!
Make me a werewolf! Make me a man-eater!
Make me a werewolf! Make me a child-eater!
I pine for blood! Human blood!
Give it to me! Give it to me tonight!
Great wolf spirit! Give it to me, and
Heart, body, and soul, I am yours.

The belief was that once the man had been transformed into a werewolf he would live as a man during the day, but be turned into a savage wolf at night. According to some traditions the spell could only be broken by stabbing the werewolf in the forehead three times, or else by the death of the man.

There are many other secret spells and chants to do with monsters. It can be very interesting also to compare legends and folk beliefs from all over the world to see what things they have in common, and in what ways they differ from each other.

Special dates and festivals

Everyone knows that there are special religious festivals each year; Christmas and Easter are the most famous. But did you know that there are also special dates and festivals that have great significance for the forces of evil and black magic? Many of these are very ancient in origin and they have become part of the folklore of many different countries. The customs and rituals associated with them are very interesting too and it is fun to collect information about them in your scrapbook. You will end up making a sort of monster's calendar if you persevere.

The only people who still celebrate these ancient festivals today are witches, and they are few and far between. But in spite of the general lack of interest in them, there are still certain times of the year when the evil powers walk abroad and when it is easiest to get in contact with them.

There are eight principal dates during the year which should feature in your monster's calendar. These are:

Candlemas	2 February
May Eve	30 April
Lammas	1 August
Hallowe'en	31 October

and:

Spring equinox around	21 March
Summer solstice around	21 June
Autumn equinox around	21 September
Winter solstice around	21 December

These last four are not specific dates, they vary from year to year. They represent the times when the length of day and night are equal (equinoxes) and also the longest and shortest days (solstices).

Long ago, when the Celtic people ruled Britain, they had other names for the first four festivals. They called Candlemas *Imbolc* or *Oimelc*; May Eve was known as *Beltane*; Lammas was *Lughnassadh*; and Hallowe'en was *Samhain*.

On these important festivals the people called on superhuman powers to help them with different aspects of their daily lives. They celebrated the first signs of spring at Candlemas, and the first signs of summer at May Eve. At Lammas they looked forward to the harvest which was just beginning, while Hallowe'en marked the beginning of winter and the time when spirits were walking abroad.

The spirits were contacted at these festivals by the ritual chanting of special spells and prayers, some of which have survived. These were like the chants made by would-be werewolves when they wanted to change into wolves.

One of the demons which was most popularly called upon was the famous horned god, the devil spirit which controlled the powers of night. This was the chant which was used to call forth this monster from the world of darkness:

By the flame that burneth bright,
O Horned One!

195

We call thy name into the night,
O Ancient One!
Thee we invoke, by the moon-led sea,
By the standing stone and the twisted tree.
Thee we invoke, where gather thy own,
By the nameless shrine forgotten and lone.
Come where the round of the dance is trod,
Horn and hoof of the goatfoot god!
By moonlit meadow, on dusky hill,
When the haunted wood is hushed and still,
Come to the charm of the chanted prayer,
As the moon bewitches the midnight air.
Evoke thy powers that potent bide
In shining stream and secret tide,
In fiery flame by starlight pale,
In shadowy host that rides the gale,
And by the fern brakes fairy-haunted
Of forests wild and woods enchanted.
Come! O come!
To the heart-beat's drum!
Come to us who gather below
When the broad white moon is climbing slow
Through the stars to the heaven's height.
We hear thy hoofs on the wind of night!
As black tree-branches shake and sigh,
By joy and terror we know thee nigh.
We speak the spell thy power unlocks
At solstice, sabbath and equinox,
Word of virtue the veil to rend,
From primal dawn to the wide world's end,

Since time began –
The blessing of Pan!
Blessed be all in hearth and hold,
Blessed all in worth more than gold,
Blessed be in strength and love,
Blessed be wherever we rove.
Vision fade not from our eyes
Of the pagan paradise
Past the gates of death and birth,
Our inheritance of earth.
From our soul the song of spring
Fade not in our wandering.
Our life with all life is one,
By blackest night or noonday sun.
Eldest of gods, on thee we call,
Blessing be on thy creatures all.

May Eve had another name which sounds much more spooky. This was Walpurgisnacht. Like Hallowe'en it was a particularly good time to contact the spirits because on both those nights the powers of evil were said to rule the earth from dusk until dawn.

However, Hallowe'en is the most important date in your monster calendar. At the start of winter it was believed that the sun went into the Underworld for a time before emerging the following spring. But it was also believed that when the doors of the Underworld opened to let in the sun, the spirits of the dead escaped as well and were free to walk the earth. So for anyone wanting to communicate with the dead, Hallowe'en was a perfect time.

This is a chant which used to be recited round the Hallowe'en bonfires, or round the large candles that burned inside the worshippers' buildings:

Fire red, summer's dead,
Yet it shall return.
Clear and bright in the night,
Burn, fire, burn.

Chorus:

Dance the ring, luck to bring,
When the year's a-turning.
Chant the rhyme at Hallows-time,
When the fire's burning.

Fire glow, vision show
Of the heart's desire,
When the spell's chanted well
Of the witching fire.

Chorus:

Dance the ring, luck to bring etc.

Fire spark, when nights are dark,
Makes our winter's mirth,
Red leaves fall, earth takes all,
Brings them to rebirth.

Chorus:

Dance the ring, luck to bring etc.

Fire fair, earth and air,
And the heaven's rain,
All blessed be, and so may we,
At Hallows-tide again.

Chorus:

Dance the ring, luck to bring etc.

See what else you can find out about Hallowe'en and other famous dates in your monster calendar. Do you know what date Frankenstein was made? Do you know when Dracula came to England? Do you know when Dr Jekyll and Mr Hyde died?

These are just some of the dates you might include in your scrapbook.

Real life monsters

You may think all the stories about monsters are too far-fetched to have any truth in them, but you would be wrong. There have been one or two frightful people in history who have really behaved like monsters. And it is because of them that the fear of monsters is more than just a ridiculous fantasy.

These are some of the most well-known real monsters. A page devoted to each of them in your scrapbook would make interesting reading alongside some of the fictional ones.

Prince Vlad Dracula

Believe it or not, he did exist. In fact he lived in part of what is now Transylvania, in Romania, during the fifteenth century.

The prince's father had been named Dracul and

by adding an 'a' to that name, his son became Dracula, which meant 'son of the devil'.

Although Vlad did not actually drink blood, as far as is known, he did have a terrible reputation for barbaric acts of cruelty.

He became known as Vlad the Impaler because of his practice of sticking his victims on top of wooden stakes so that they died a slow, agonising death. He also used to cook his victims alive, and even fed them to their unsuspecting families. He used to hold huge massacres after his battles, and on one occasion he ordered three hundred prisoners to be burned alive.

In the end he was beheaded himself, though not before he had killed enough to go down in history as one of the most bloodthirsty rulers that ever lived. And of course now you will understand how the vampire monster came to be called Dracula.

Arnold Paole

Some three hundred years after Vlad the Impaler terrorised Transylvania, a real vampire stalked the neighbouring state of Serbia.

This vampire was called Arnold Paole. He had lived a perfectly normal life until he was bitten by a vampire one night. Then he knew that he would become a vampire himself unless he could find the one that had attacked him and kill it.

Luckily, he succeeded in carrying out this cure and all seemed well at first. However, Arnold was accidentally killed and within a month of his death villagers started to see him walking round the village at night. The vampire had risen! Then within a few days of Arnold's appearance four people died in the village – victims of the vampire.

It was decided to open Arnold's grave and, ten weeks after his burial, his coffin was opened in the presence of three doctors and two army officers. The sight that met their eyes was horrifying. Arnold's hair and nails had grown. His eyes and mouth were wide open, fresh blood covered his lips and there was no sign of decay in his body; he looked like a living man. There was no doubt about it: Arnold Paole had become a vampire.

To kill the vampire once and for all, Arnold's corpse was scattered with garlic and a wooden stake was driven into his heart with one blow. Warm blood gushed from the wound, the body twisted in agony and let out a dreadful cry.

Then the bodies of Arnold's victims were dealt with in a similar way, to prevent them from becoming vampires themselves. And as a last measure all the vampire bodies were thrown onto a huge bonfire, because once a vampire's soul had lost its body it was forced to go to the underworld.

The great horror stories

Most of the greatest monsters come from famous horror stories. Many of these as we have seen have been used to make films and television plays, but these adaptations have often changed the original story, and they are sometimes less exciting and less terrifying than the originals. After all, your imagination is far more creative when you are reading a story than when you are watching a film; and this is why there are few things more frightening than reading a gripping horror story on a dark, stormy night, all alone in your bedroom after everyone else has fallen fast asleep.

There are many good horror stories but here are thirteen (you're not superstitious, are you?) of the most well known that you might like to start with. As with the films, write down your opinion of each story when you read it. Keep a record in your scrapbook so that if you ever read the stories again you can compare your impressions of them. It is interesting, too, to see in what way the stories have been changed in the films. And of course reading these stories will take you back to the opening pages of the scrapbook, because you will almost certainly want to start writing your own horror stories after reading these. In alphabetical order of the author's surnames they are:

Bierce, Ambrose – *The Damned Thing*
Crawford, F. Marion – *The Witch of Prague*
Endore, Guy – *The Werewolf of Paris*
James, Henry – *The Turn of the Screw*
James, M. R. – *'Oh, Whistle and I'll Come to You My Lad'*
Kipling, Rudyard – *At The End of the Passage*
Le Fanu, Sheridan – *Uncle Silas*
Leroux, Gaston – *The Phantom of the Opera*
Poe, Edgar Allan – *The Tell-tale Heart*
Shelley, Mary – *Frankenstein*
Stevenson, Robert Louis – *The Strange Case of Dr Jekyll and Mr Hyde*
Stoker, Bram – *Dracula*
Wilde, Oscar – *The Picture of Dorian Gray*

GHASTLY RHYMES

Insulting Behaviour

(Starts the fun!)

Happy birthday to you!
Squashed tomatoes and stew;
Bread and butter in the gutter,
Happy birthday to you!

Every time it rains
I think of you:
Drip . . . drip . . . drip . . .

The rain makes everything beautiful;
It makes the flowers blue.
If the rain makes everything beautiful
Why doesn't it rain on you?

Roses are red, cabbages are green,
My face is funny, but yours is a scream.

Roses are red, violets are blue;
Onions stink, and so do you.

Go on to college, gather your knowledge,
Study and worry and stew.
If they make penicillin from mouldy cheese
They can make something good out of you.

Grow up, grow up.
Every time I look at you
I throw up.

Your father is a baker,
Your mother cuts the bread;
And you're the little doughnut
With a hole right through your head!

208

I wish I were a dozen eggs
Sitting in a tree,
And when you passed along below
I'd splatter you with me.

That's the way to the zoo.
That's the way to the zoo.
The monkey's house is nearly full
But there's room enough for you.

209

Back to School

(Let's hiss and boo!)

Latin is a language
As dead as dead can be;
First it killed the Romans
And now it's killing me.

Julius Caesar
The Roman geezer
Squashed his wife
With a lemon squeezer.

Land of soapy water,
Teacher's having a bath;
Headmaster's looking through the keyhole,
Having a jolly good laugh.

We break up, we break down,
We don't care if the school falls down.
This time next week where shall we be?
Out of the gates of misery!
No more Latin, no more French,
No more sitting on the hard old bench.
No more cabbages filled with slugs,
No more drinking out of dirty old mugs.
No more spiders in my tea,
Making googly eyes at me.
Kick up tables, kick up chairs,
Kick the teacher down the stairs,
If that does not serve her right,
Blow her up with dynamite.

You go to school dinners,
You sit side by side,
You cannot escape –
Though many have tried.
You look at the gravy,
All lumpy and still,
If that doesn't get you
The custard will.

If you stay to school dinners
Better throw them aside;
A lot of kids didn't,
A lot of kids died.

The meat is made of iron,
The spuds are made of steel;
And if that don't get you
The afters will!

I love to do my homework,
It makes me feel so good.
I love to do exactly
As my teacher says I should.

I love to do my homework
I never miss a day.
I even love the men in white
Who are taking me away.

'Stupid boy! Where are elephants found?'
The pompous teacher bossed.
'They're never found!' the child replied,
'They're too big to get lost.'

When I die bury me deep;
Bury my history book at my feet.
Tell the teacher I've gone to rest
And won't be back for the history test.

No more pencils, no more books,
No more teachers' ugly looks,
No more things that bring us sorrow
'Cos we won't be here tomorrow.

Feeding Time

(Grub's up!)

I eat my peas with honey;
I've done it all my life.
It makes the peas taste funny
But it keeps them on the knife.

Mary ate jam,
Mary ate jelly,
Mary went home
With a pain in her –
Don't be mistaken,
Don't be misled,
Mary went home
With a pain in her head

Robin the Bobbin, the big-bellied Ben,
He ate more meat than fourscore men;
He ate a cow, he ate a calf,
He ate a butcher and a half,
He ate a church, he ate a steeple,
He ate the priest and all the people!

A cannibal bold of Penzance
Ate an uncle and two of his aunts,
A cow and a calf,
An ox and a half –
And now he can't button his pants!

There was an old lady of Ryde
Who ate some bad apples and died.
The apples fermented
Inside the lamented
And made cider inside her inside.

There was a queer fellow named Woodin
Who always ate pepper with puddin',
Till, one day, 'tis said,
He sneezed off his head!
That imprudent old fellow named Woodin.

Cuthbert Bede

Nobody loves me, everybody hates me;
I'm going to the garden to eat worms.
Long thin slimy ones, short fat fuzzy ones,
Ooey gooey ooey gooey worms.

The long thin slimy ones slip down easily;
The short fat fuzzy ones stick.
Nobody likes me, everybody hates me;
I'm going to the garden to be sick.

You bite off the heads and suck out the juice
And throw the skins away;
Nobody knows how I survive
On a hundred worms a day.

There was an Old Person of Ewell,
Who chiefly subsisted on gruel;
But to make it more nice
He inserted some mice,
Which refreshed that Old Person of Ewell.

Edward Lear

There was an Old Person whose habits
Induced him to feed upon rabbits;
When he'd eaten eighteen
He turned perfectly green,
Upon which he relinquished those habits.

Edward Lear

Animal Crackers

(Beastly stuff, this!)

A farmer once called his cow Zephyr
She seemed such a breezy young hephyr
When the farmer drew near
She kicked off his ear
And now the old farmer's much dephyr.

Radi was a circus lion,
Radi was a woman-hater,
Radi had a lady trainer,
Radiator.

Algy met a bear,
The bear met Algy.
The bear was bulgy,
The bulge was Algy.

If you build a better mousetrap
And put it in your house,
Before long, Mother Nature's
Going to build a better mouse.

There was a dachshund once, so long,
He hadn't any notion
How long it took to notify
His tail of his emotion;
And so it happened, while his eyes
Were filled with woe and sadness,
His little tail went wagging on
Because of previous gladness.

Our little dog
Is a terrible sinner –
He slinks up to the table
And tries to pinch dinner.

Thin Dog

I've got a dog as thin as a rail,
He's got fleas all over his tail;
Every time his tail goes flop,
The fleas on the bottom all hop to the top.

Great fleas have little fleas upon their backs to
bite 'em
And little fleas have lesser fleas, and so ad
infinitum;
The great fleas themselves in turn have greater
fleas to go on,
While these again have greater still, and greater
still, and so on.

Some folks say that fleas are black,
But I know that's not so,
'Cause Mary had a little lamb
With fleas as white as snow.

Curious fly
Vinegar jug
Slippery edge
Pickled bug.

I wish I were a little grub
With whiskers round my tummy;
I'd climb into a honey pot
And make my tummy gummy.

A centipede was happy quite,
Until a frog, in fun,
Said, 'Pray, which leg comes after which?'
This raised her mind to such a pitch
She lay distracted in a ditch
Considering how to run.

Ipsy Wipsy spider
Crawling up the spout,
Down came the rain
And washed the spider out;
Out came the sunshine,
Dried up all the rain,
Ipsy Wipsy spider
Went up the spout again.

Little Miss Muffet
Sat on her tuffet,
Eating her Irish stew.
Along came a spider
And sat down beside her,
So she ate him up too.

There's a long, long worm a-crawling
Across the roof of my tent.
I can hear the whistle calling,
And it's time that I went.
There's the cold, cold water waiting
For me to take my morning dip,
And when I come back I'll find that worm
Upon my pillow-slip.

Raising frogs for profit
Is a very sorry joke.
How can you make money
When so many of them croak?

One, two, three
Me mother caught a flea.
Put it in the teapot
To make a cup of tea.

A sea-serpent saw a big tanker,
Bit a hole in her side and then sank her.
It swallowed the crew
In a minute or two,
And then picked its teeth with the anchor.

Heart to Heart

(Slush, gush and mush!)

He spoke the Truth

'Your teeth are like the stars,' he said
And pressed her hand so white.
He spoke the truth, for like the stars,
Her teeth came out at night!

I love you, I love you,
Be my valentine.
And give me your bubble gum –
You're sitting on mine.

I love you, I love you,
I love you so well,
If I had a peanut
I'd give you the shell.

Ruth and Johnnie

Ruth and Johnnie
Side by side,
Went out for an
Auto ride.
They hit a bump,
Ruth hit a tree,
And John kept going
Ruthlessly.

'Twas in a restaurant they met,
Romeo and Juliet.
He had no cash to pay the debt,
So Romeo'd while Juliet.

I know a girl named Passion.
I asked her for a date.
I took her out to dinner
And gosh! How Passionate!

I remember – I remember well –
The first girl that I kissed.
She closed her eyes, I closed mine,
And then – worst luck – we missed!

A pair in a hammock
Attempted to kiss,
And in less than a jiffy
They landed like this.

'Tis better to have loved
And lost
Than wed and be
Forever bossed.

Family Fun

(Relatively ghastly!)

Pop Bottles Pop-bottles

Pop bottles pop-bottles
In pop shops;
The pop-bottles Pop bottles
Poor Pop drops.

When Pop drops pop-bottles
Pop-bottles plop!
Pop-bottle-tops topple
Pop mops slop!

I had written to Aunt Maud
Who was on a trip abroad,
When I heard she'd died of cramp
Just too late to save the stamp.

An accident happened to my brother Jim
When somebody threw a tomato at him –
Tomatoes are juicy and don't hurt the skin,
But this one was specially packed in a tin.

Speak roughly to your little boy,
And beat him when he sneezes;
He only does it to annoy
Because he knows it teases.

Lewis Carroll

Little Jerry

For asking lots of questions
Little Jerry has a flair.
His weary parents say he is
Their little question heir.

Baby and I
Were baked in a pie,
The gravy was wonderful hot.
We had nothing to pay
To the baker that day
And so we crept out of the pot.

Rock-a-bye, baby,
In the treetop.
Don't you fall out –
It's a very big drop.

People and Pastimes

**(Yes, it's the magnificent
Chapter Seven!)**

There was an odd fellow of Tyre
Who constantly sat on the fire.
When asked, 'Are you hot?'
He said, 'Certainly not,'
I'm James Winterbottom, Esquire.'

Good Manners

Charlotte, having seen his body,
Borne before her on a shutter,
Like a well-conducted person
Went on cutting bread and butter.

W. M. Thackeray

A maiden caught stealing a dahlia,
Said, 'Oh, you shan't tell on me, shahlia?'
But the florist who caught her
Said, 'You shouldn't have oughter,
They'll send you to jail, you bad gahlia.'

Sam, Sam, the dirty man,
Washed his face in the frying pan;
Combed his hair with a donkey's tail,
And scratched his belly with his big toenail.

from 'The English Struwwelpeter'

Shock-headed Peter! There he stands,
With his horrid hair and hands.
See, his nails are never cut;
They are grim'd as black as soot'
And, the sloven, I declare,
He has never comb'd his hair;
Anything to me is sweeter,
Than to see Shock-headed Peter.

*Dr Heinrich Hoffman, translated by
J. R. Planché*

On the Four Georges

*George the First was always reckoned
Vile – but viler George the Second;
And what mortal ever heard
Any good of George the Third?
When from earth the Fourth descended,
God be praised, the Georges ended.*

W. S. Landor

from 'The Mad Gardener's Song'

He thought he saw an Elephant,
That practised on a fife:
He looked again, and found it was
A letter from his wife.
'At length I realise,' he said,
'The bitterness of Life!'

He thought he saw a Buffalo
Upon the chimney piece:
He looked again, and found it was
His Sister's Husband's Niece.
'Unless you leave this house,' he said,
'I'll send for the Police!'

Lewis Carroll

I am a girl guide dressed in blue,
These are the actions I can do –
Salute the captain,
Curtsey to the queen,
Show my panties to the football team.

There lived an old man in a garret,
So afraid of a little tom-cat,
That he pulled himself up to the ceiling,
And hung himself up on his hat.

And for fear of the wind and the rain
He took his umbrella to bed –
I've half an idea that silly old man
Was a little bit wrong in the head.

When, in frosty midnight,
He cruises through the air,
What Santa needs for Christmas
Is fur-lined underwear.

But when sliding down the chimney
Towards the fire that we tend
Asbestos pants for Santa
Would be better in the end.

Good King Wenceslas looked out
On the Feast of Stephen;
A snowball hit him on the snout
And made it all uneven.
Brightly shone his conk that night,
And the pain was cruel,
Till a doctor came in sight,
Riding on a mu-oo-el.

While shepherds washed their socks by night
All boiling in the pot
A lump of soot came rolling down
And spoilt the blooming lot.

All Shapes and Sizes

(Laughs little and large!)

A girl who weighed many an oz
Used language I dare not pronoz
When a fellow unkind
Pulled her chair out behind
Just to see, so he said, if she'd boz.

A sleeper from the Amazon
Put nighties of his grandma's on.
The reason? That
He was too fat
To get his own pyjamas on.

A young man of fair Aberdeen
Once grew so remarkably lean,
So flat and compressed,
That his back touched his chest,
And sideways he couldn't be seen.

Pete, Pete, is always neat
From the top of his head to the soles of his feet;
He hasn't got any hair at all,
So he buffs his bonce like a billiard ball.

Said the toe to the sock,
'Let me through, let me through.'
Said the sock to the toe,
'I'll be darned if I do.'

Moses supposes
His toeses are roses
But Moses supposes erroneously.
For nobody's toeses
Are posies of roses
As Moses supposes his toeses to be.

Epitaph on a Marf

Wot a marf 'e'd got,
Wot a marf.
When 'e was a kid,
Goo 'Lor'luv'll
'Is pore old muvver
Must 'a'fed 'im wiv a shuvvle.

Wot a gap 'e'd got,
Pore chap.
'E'd never been known to larf,
Cos if 'e did
It's a penny to a quid
'E'd 'a' split 'is fice in 'arf.

A lady from over the Channel
Once washed with a very cold flannel.
It totally froze
Her poor little nose,
And made it as hard as enamel.

There was a young lady named Rose
Who had a large wart on her nose.
When she had it removed
Her appearance improved
But her glasses slipped down to her toes.

It doesn't breathe; it doesn't smell;
It doesn't feel so very well.
I am disgusted with my nose –
The only thing it does is blows.

Sick and Sorry

(This'll have you in stitches!)

Germ Warfare

I shot a sneeze into the air.
It fell to earth, I know not where.
But some time later, so I'm told,
Twenty others caught my cold.

There was a young lady of Spain
Who was dreadfully sick on a train
Not once, but again
And again and again
And again and again and again.

There was a young lady of Twickenham
Whose boots were too tight to walk quickenham.
She walked for a mile
And stopped at a stile
And pulled them both off and was sickenham.

Doctor Bell fell down the well
And broke his collar-bone.
Doctors should attend the sick
And leave the well alone.

Llewelyn Peter James Maguire
Touched a live electric wire;
Back on his heels it sent him rocking –
His language (like the wire) was shocking.

There was a young lady of Riga,
Who rode with a smile on a tiger;
They returned from the ride
With the lady inside
And the smile on the face of the tiger.

Humpty Dumpty sat on a wall,
Humpty Dumpty had a great fall.
All the king's horses and all the king's men
Had scrambled eggs for breakfast again.

Connie, Connie, in the tub,
She forgot to use the plug.
Oh, my heavens! Oh, my soul!
There goes Connie down the hole!
Glub, glub, glub . . . .

He rocked the boat,
Did Ezra Shrank,
These bubbles mark
                o
                o
                o
                o
                o
                o
Where Ezra sank.

'Tis easy enough to be pleasant,
When life flows by with a whistle,
But the man worthwhile
Is the man with a smile,
When he sits down on a thistle.

There once was an old man called Keith
Who mislaid his pair of false teeth –
Laid them on a chair,
Forgot they were there,
Sat down and was bitten beneath.

There was a man of Thessaly.
And he was wondrous wise,
He jumped into a bramble bush
And scratched out both his eyes.
And when he saw his eyes were out,
With all his might and main
He jumped into another bush
And scratched them in again.

There was an old soldier of Bicester
Who was walking one day with his sister,
When a cow, at one poke,
Tossed her into an oak,
Before the old gentleman missed her.

A man and his lady-love, Min,
Skated out where the ice was quite thin.
Had a quarrel, no doubt,
For I hear they fell out:
What a blessing they didn't fall in!

Little Willie;
Pair of skates;
Hole in the ice;
Pearly gates.

The manner of her death was thus –
She was druv over by a bus.

Bessie met a bus,
The bus met Bessie,
The bus was messy,
The mess was Bessie.

The curfew tolls the knell of parting day,
A line of cars winds slowly o'er the lea,
A pedestrian plods his absent-minded way
And leaves the world quite unexpectedly.

There was an old woman of Clewer
Who was riding a bike and it threw her.
A butcher came by,
And said, 'Missus, don't cry,'
And he fastened her on with a skewer.

Her death it brought us bitter woe –
Yea, to the heart it wrung us;
And all because she didn't know
A mushroom from a fungus.

Willie's Little Ways

Willie poisoned his father's tea;
Father died in agony.
Mother came, and looked quite vexed:
'Really, Will,' she said, 'what next?'

Into the family's drinking well
Willie pushed his sister Nell.
She's there yet, because it kilt her –
Now we'll have to buy a filter.

Willie, with a thirst for gore,
Nailed his sister to the door.
Mother said, with humour quaint:
'Willie dear, don't scratch the paint.'

Little Willie, late one night,
Lit a stick of dynamite,
Don't you think he had a cheek?
It's been raining Willie for a week.

Little Willie from his mirror
Licked the mercury all off,
Thinking, in his childish error,
It would cure his whooping cough.
At the funeral Willie's mother
Smartly said to Mrs Brown:
"'Twas a chilly day for Willie
When the mercury went down.'

Little Willie in the best of sashes
Played with the fire and was burnt to ashes.
Now, although the room grows chilly,
We haven't the heart to poke poor Willie.

258

Willie in the cauldron fell;
See the grief on his mother's brow!
Mother loved her darling well;
Darling's quite hard-boiled by now.

Ghastly – and Ghostly

(It's spooktacular!)

In a dark, dark wood, there was a dark, dark
  house,
And in that dark, dark house, there was a dark,
  dark room,
And in that dark, dark room, there was a dark,
  dark cupboard,
And in that dark, dark cupboard, there was a
  dark, dark shelf,
And in that dark, dark shelf, there was a dark,
  dark box,
And in that dark, dark box, there was a **GHOST!**

Eerie Men of Erith

There are men in the village of Erith
Whom nobody seeth or heareth,
And there looms on the marge
Of the river a barge
That nobody roweth or steereth.

There once was a phantom named Pete,
Who never would play, drink or eat.
He said, 'I don't care
For a Coke or eclair –
Can't you see that I'm dead on my feet?'

The Ghost's Lament

Woe's me, woe's me,
The acorn's not yet
Fallen from the tree,
That's to grow the oak
That's to make the cradle,
That's to rock the bairn,
That's to grow a man
That's to lay me.

A Witch's Spell

Hinx, minx, the old witch winks,
The fat begins to fry.
Nobody at home but jumping Joan,
Father, mother and I.
Stick, stock, stone dead,
Blind man can't see;
Every man will have a slave,
You and I must be he.

The Giant

Fee, fie, fo, fum!
I smell the blood of an Englishman.
Be he alive, or be he dead,
I'll grind his bones to make my bread.

There's a Thought

(Truth will out!)

If all the world were paper,
And all the seas were ink;
And all the trees were bread and cheese,
What should we do for drink?

Wonders of Modern Science

Twinkle, twinkle, little star,
I don't wonder what you are:
You're the cooling down of gases
Forming into solid masses.

Don't worry if your life's a joke,
And your successes few;
Remember that the mighty oak
Was once a nut like you!

Twixt optimist and pessimist
The difference is droll;
The optimist sees the doughnut,
The pessimist sees the hole.

All things have savour, though some very
    small,
Nay, a box on the ear hath no smell at all.

It's hard to lose a friend
When your heart is full of hope;
But it's worse to lose a towel
When your eyes are full of soap.

Old Law

The law doth punish man or woman
Who steals the goose from off the common,
But lets the greater felon loose
That steals the common from the goose.

The rain it raineth on the just
And on the unjust fella
But more on the just than the unjust
'Cause the unjust hath the just's umbrella.

Yes, every poet is a fool;
By demonstration Ned can show it:
Happy, could Ned's inverted rule
Prove every fool a poet.

Matthew Prior

*Swans sing before they die – 'twere no bad
 thing
Should certain persons die before they sing.*

S. T. Coleridge

The Wishes of an Elderly Man (At a garden-party, June 1914)

I wish I loved the Human Race;
I wish I loved its silly face;
I wish I liked the way it walks;
I wish I liked the way it talks;
And when I'm introduced to one
I wish I thought **What Jolly Fun!**

Walter Raleigh

Wishing on a Star

Starlight, star bright,
First star I see tonight,
I wish I may, I wish I might –
Oh, nuts, it's just a satellite.

Starlight, star bright,
First star I see tonight,
I'd like to fly, I'd like to go –
Oh, nuts, it's just a UFO . . .

Ghastly Groaners

(Unlucky for you!)

Newton heard a sort of plonk –
An apple fell upon his conk.
Discovered gravitation law,
It shook old Isaac to the core.

Little Jack Horner sat in a corner
Eating his Christmas pie.
He put in his thumb, but instead of a plum,
He squirted fruit juice in his eye.

Sweet little Eileen Rose
Was tired and sought some sweet repose
But her sister Clare
Put a pin on her chair
And sweet little Eileen Rose!

There was an old man from Dunoon,
Who always ate soup with a fork,
For he said, 'As I eat
Neither fish, fowl nor flesh,
I should finish my dinner too quick.'

269

A painter who lived in West Ditting
Interrupted two girls with their knitting.
He said with a sigh,
'That park bench – well, I
Just painted it, right where you're sitting!'

Jack and Jill went up the hill,
To fetch a pail of water.
Jack fell down and broke his crown,
And sued the farmer and his daughter.

When good King Arthur ruled this land.
He was a goodly king;
He stole three pecks of barley meal,
To make a bag-pudding.

A bag-pudding the king did make,
And stuff'd it well with plums;
And in it put great lumps of fat,
As big as my two thumbs.

The king and queen did eat thereof,
And noblemen beside;
And what they could not eat that night,
The queen next morning fried.

Papa Moses killed a skunk;
Mama Moses cooked the skunk;
Baby Moses ate the skunk;
My, oh my, how they stunk!

Here I sit in the moonlight,
Abandoned by women and men,
Muttering over and over,
'I'll never eat garlic again.'

I shot an arrow in the air
It fell to earth, I know not where.
I lose all my arrows that way.

Down the street his funeral goes
As sobs and wails diminish,
He died from drinking varnish,
But he had a lovely finish.

Last Laughs: Epitaphs

(What a way to go!)

Grave Note

In this chapter all the epitaphs marked with a star are authentic ones, first seen on genuine tombstones in real churchyards.

Here lies a man who met his fate
Because he put on too much weight.
To over-eating he was prone
But now he's gained his final **STONE.**

* At Great Torrington, Devon

Here lies a man who was killed by lightning;
He died when his prospects seemed to be
  brightening;
He might have cut a flash in this world of
  trouble,
But the flash cut him, and he lies in the stubble.

Old Tom is gone (too soon, alas!)
He tried to trace escaping gas.
With lighted match he braved the fates
Which blew him to the Pearly Gates.

The bomb he set went off too soon,
And here his story ceases.
The bits they found are buried here –
And thus he Rests in Pieces.

*Underneath this pile of stones
Lies all that's left of Sally Jones.
Her name was Briggs, it was not Jones,
But Jones was used to rhyme with stones.*

Beneath these stones repose the bones
Of Theodosius Grim;
He took his beer from year to year,
And then the bier took him.

A Brewer

*Here lies poor Burton,
He was both hale and stout;
Death laid him on his bitter bier,
Now in another world he hops about.*

* At Upton-On-Severn

Beneath this stone in hopes of Zion
Doth lie the landlord of the Lion;
His son keeps on the business still,
Resigned unto the heavenly will.

* On Meredith, Organist at Oxford

Here lies one blown out of breath
Who lived a merry life, and died a Merideth.

* On Leslie Moore

Here lies what's left
Of Leslie Moore –
No Les
No more.

Beneath this silent stone is laid
A noisy antiquated maid,
Who from her cradle talked till death,
And ne'er before was out of breath.

* Here lies my wife:
Here let her lie!
Now she's at rest,
And so am I.

> *John Dryden*

Here lies a woman, no man can deny it,
She died in peace, although she lived unquiet;
Her husband prays, if e'er this way you walk,
You would tread softly – if she wake she'll talk.

Here lies the mother of children seven,
Four on earth and three in Heaven;
The three in Heaven preferring rather
To die with mother than live with father.

* Nettlebed Churchyard, Oxfordshire

Here lies father, and mother, and sister, and I;
We all died within the space of one short year.
They were all buried at Wimble except I,
And I be buried here.

Andrew Gear of Sunderland

Here lies the body of Andrew Gear,
Whose mouth did stretch from ear to ear;
Stranger, step lightly o'er his head,
For if he gapes, by Josh, you're dead.

Sacred to the Memory of Maria
(To Say Nothing of Jane and Martha) Sparks

Stranger, pause and drop a tear,
For Susan Sparks lies buried here:
Mingled in some perplexing manner,
With Jane, Maria, and portions of Hannah.

Max Adeler

Here rests the body of our MP
Who promised lots for you and me.
His words his deeds did not fulfil
And though he's dead he's **LYING STILL.**

Bill Muffet said
His car couldn't skid;
This monument shows
That it could and did.

On Sir John Vanbrugh, Architect

Under this stone, reader, survey
Dead Sir John Vanbrugh's house of clay,
Lie heavy on him, earth! for he
Laid many heavy loads on thee.

Abel Evans

He passed the bobby without any fuss,
And he passed a cart of hay,
He tried to pass a swerving bus,
And then he passed away.

In crossing o'er the fatal bridge
John Morris he was slain.
But it was not by any mortal hand
But by a railway train.

Here lies a chump who got no gain
From jumping on a moving train.
Banana skins on platform seven
Ensured his terminus was Heaven.

Here lies the body of our Anna
Done to death by a banana.
It wasn't the fruit that laid her low
But the skin of the thing that made her go.

Index of First Lines

283